Anonymous

From Pillar to Post

A Novel

Anonymous

From Pillar to Post
A Novel

ISBN/EAN: 9783337032982

Printed in Europe, USA, Canada, Australia, Japan

Cover: Foto ©Andreas Hilbeck / pixelio.de

More available books at **www.hansebooks.com**

FROM PILLAR TO POST.

A Novel.

LONDON:

TINSLEY BROTHERS, 18, CATHERINE ST., STRAND.

1864.

LONDON :
BRADBURY AND EVANS, PRINTERS, WHITEFRIARS.

CONTENTS.

CHAPTER I.

PAGE

GOOD — BAD — INDIFFERENT .   .   1

CHAPTER II.

A PRETTY STORY ! .   ‘   33

CHAPTER III.

CONFESSIO AMANTIS. LADY HARBLEDOWN STARTS BLANCHE.
HER RIVAL'S PEDIGREE 65

CHAPTER IV.

A CARD PARTY—A HEART TURNS UP   .   . 100

CHAPTER V.

LOVE IN A COTTAGE . .   118

CHAPTER VI.

A QUEER MEETING—A CRASH .   .   . 130

CHAPTER VII.

NOT MERE TALK—PALLIDA MORS .   145

CHAPTER VIII.

BRAVING IT OUT   173

CHAPTER IX.

A GAME OF HAZARD—THE LAST STAKE   197

CHAPTER X.

PAGE

OLD FACES.—BLACKLOCK'S STORY .   224

CHAPTER XI.

A REQUEST REFUSED.—ANOTHER GRANTED .   .   . 245

CHAPTER XII.

TRAVELLING COMPANIONS.—ALL OVER   .   .   . 254

CHAPTER XIII.

THE ENDING OF THE LANE   . . 273

CHAPTER XIV.

THE SERPENT'S SEED CRUSHED   .   .   304

FROM PILLAR TO POST.

CHAPTER I.

GOOD—BAD—INDIFFERENT.

IF, in the first flush of summer, a young fellow
rent chambers in the Temple or the Albany; if
he can occupy three or four hours a-day in the
pursuit of some self-imposed purpose, yet do
not live in the dread of intermediate sessions,
an ill-timed dissolution, or the sudden calling
out of a patriotic militia; if he have, say 200*l.*
a year clear, with 100*l.* more a year in credit;
and if, to conclude, the town be only full, the
sun will only shine, and he have only found
lavender-coloured gloves to fit him without a
crease—I know not what is left for him to
desire. He is *Dis carus ipsis, quippe ter qua-
terque,* and can receive nothing further even

from the bountiful *dona-Ferentes*. And it is a miserable world! I think not, my good friends. But the preacher said so as recently as Sunday forenoon last! Yes, I heard him, and have little doubt I shall hear him say the same thing Sunday forenoon next, if I have the happiness of escorting you to church. But all *I* can say is, that in the interval—last night only—I saw our reverend mourner prove himself as jolly an old soul as ever sipped Sauterne, chuckled at a good joke, won the odd trick, or pocketed the pool. A miserable world? Bah!

It was the summit of the season. Her Majesty's was crammed. There was to be a new opera, and a new *danseuse*. For once, brothers did not vote the singing a bore—for once, sisters had no desire to leave before the ballet; they accommodated each others' taste in order to be able to gratify their own. Nothing like the urgency of compromise. Young ladies tell you they have a " passion " for music: would they be horrified if young fellows avowed a " passion " for *pas-seuls*?

The horse-shoe tiers were adorned—and not

a break in all the rows—with the handsomest
busts of the handsomest race you can show me
anywhere the whole world through. You prefer
fresh faces about half-past eight A.M., faces
glowing from tossed-off slumber and the bracing
energies of the bath, looking at you across white
damask and a breakfast-table. We will not quarrel
about that. But tell me, if in the house this night,
there be a nearer approach to the "Idalian Aphro-
dite beautiful" than Mabel Lady Harbledown?
See; look along the second tier—do you notice
the centre box, which the girl with the warm
golden hair is leaning out of? Well, further
from us—to the right—one, two, fourth box
from it; she leans forward. Yes, that is she.
" By Jove ! "—You may well say, " By Jove ! "
Look at her well. Here are the lorgnettes ;
take them, quick !

Say she is twenty-seven. May be : more,
certainly not. Splendid as she is, I think she
is improving still. You can see her to the waist
only ; but the fear of Horace lest—

"Desinat in piscem mulier formosa supernè"—

will not apply ; depend on it, *that* woman is

D 2

not dolphin downwards. And what you see, can you criticise? Find me a fault. I fear the turn of that head has turned many another; and the whiteness—I will not liken it to marble —of that perhaps hard face has more than once been said to induce in other faces the colour which is ascribed to envy. Perhaps *hard* face. Have I recalled the word? Yes; for as I spoke, she turned her eyes full towards me, and those eyes completely save her. Strange to see in such a chiselled countenance, under such dark proud lashes, such rapid, revelling, glad eyes; eyes with not a spark of pride, eyes with not a thought of coldness in them—at least as I see them now—and they are only vagrant about the house. Her eyes look outward. All eyes do! No, pardon me, they do not; look again, for you are assuredly mistaken. Nothing more common than more or less, and sometimes altogether (physical as well as mental), introverted vision. And so, I say, hers looked significantly outward. Like a Tyrolese sharp-shooter was she; nothing could live within the horizon of her vision. Down

upon it at once. Attempt not Delphic signals
and telegraphic love-passages within her gaze,
if you would not have her see you. "My
dear!" she will say to you afterwards, "I saw
it all; but I will not tell. The fairies befriend
you!" Kind, conscious Mabel! Tell! I never
knew her do it.

And the boy who sits with her, who alone
sits with her; he does not seem to appreciate
his privilege as he should. "Cornet of Light
Dragoons" is stamped upon him; see it in the
shirt-front, see it in his studs—nay, I know not
where you would not see it. You would be dull
indeed to miss it. He is not in love with Lady
Harbledown. That perhaps is strange; but,
what is much stranger, he is not in love with
himself either. He is clearly of opinion that an
opera-box is a good thing; that well-turned
boots are a good thing; that sitting near so
handsome a woman is a good thing; in fact,
that life generally is a good thing. He is a
philosopher, without at all striving to be so;
and is wise in his way without having been
tutored to it either by study or suffering.

Listless, he is not ; yet he never moves without strict urgency. Neither is he stupid, though he never speaks to fill up a pause, and is not in the least disconcerted by a prolonged symphony of silence. Light Dragoon though he is, and unmistakeably is, he respects the alphabet, and recognises the letter "r," despite its having been cut by the regiment, and dismissed the service generally. If he is not a right good fellow, faces are as false as words.

"He never used to be so late as this. I wonder what keeps him. And when he has not seen me for eight months!"

"If your ladyship knew the lectures I have received from him, in our younger days, for being a couple of minutes behind time. Do you think I shall know him? See ; the overture begins. He will lose it."

A wave of the *bâton*, and the house is hushed. Another, and Genius speaks through a hundred instruments to three thousand listeners. The poor author lacks this precious privilege. The dull, synonymous with the many, can be even momentarily inspired only by the aggregated

enthusiasm of their kind; and to comprehend
the utterances of the inspired, galvanic inspiration at least is demanded. A multitude has
electric intercommunication, just as proximate
trees shake each other. Few people have complete self-sufficient natures, and are frantic in
their solitude. In fact, such are themselves the
inspired.

The first act closes amid plentiful plaudits;
but Lady Harbledown and the young Cornet
are still alone. They are talking, and with
sufficient cheerfulness; but the remarks are not
brilliant enough for you and me. How should
they be? One of the speakers wants nothing;
and the other, his fair companion to-night, wants
somebody else, who comes not—the ungallant!
For conversation to be memorable, the inter-
locutors must have a purpose—cross-purposes
are best. *Then*, under skilful management, talk
grows into the dramatic, and does for to-morrow's meditation. I wonder if any such is
astir within the house just now. Since these
two will not yield us profit, we must go
a-wandering.

Suppose we halt at the box corresponding on the left to the one we have just quitted on the right. The conversation may be neither epigrammatic nor very didactic; but there is plenty of it. Its female occupant lacks not satellites, though, for anything you and I know, she too may be thinking of a lost pleiad. She is well screened from the gaze of all save those who are so willingly imprisoned with her : and accepts *their* gaze with a quiet indifference that does not even rise to the dignity of disdain. But they continue to bestow it, for, having chosen to crown her queen, they must maintain their homage. Twenty is a young age at which to sit there and be careless of compliments; and she has not long stepped out of her teens. She has the figure, the height, but not the *hauteur* of an embodied Juno—or, perhaps, Juno without her fulness, for she is slender in her easily-worn stateliness. Her close brown hair is worn with the perfection of plainness : no wreath, no coronet. From a Gothic chain round her lithe neck falls a Gothic pendant on her full, frailly-guarded bust : all gold—not a

jewel in it. Blue enamel mixes with the bright
metal in the single bracelets—but again no
stones : gems are permitted only on the fingers.
One glove is momentarily off; and if what
Byron says be true, that the "fair symmetry of
limbs" may be guessed by their "terminating
so well," the enigma of her hidden form is
solved. Certainly were I a sculptor, I would
have that head ; were I an artist, I would have
that brown hair, those brown eyes, that nose,
straight, but full at the nostrils, that compact
mouth and chin; nor would I bate one shade of
colour from that complexion, dark—dark as a
deep pool is dark—from the profundity of her
nature. "Splendid girl!" most would say ;
"somewhat of the she-tiger in her." They
would not know her. *We* will. They call her
Lettice Tallington.

Do those five—six—men and boys amuse
her ? Does she entertain them? I don't know.
They like to be there : their being there proves
it ; and she has little option. If you asked her
opinion about our sex, and she were frank with
you, she would tell you that we are "fools."

She has good reason to think so. There they sit, and stand, and loll, and stare at her, and utter ineffable nonsense, and would venture on impertinence would she only allow it. She forbids their originality ; so, though they say much, they are not the less dull. What can she do ? She can look handsome at them : she can labour to bandy badinage with them : she must labour, for the wit is so poor. That done, she can admire her frail fan ; she can admire her costly white silk skirt ; she can wrap her long full white mohair cloak more closely about her, and then let it fall negligently in skilful folds about her throne. She can look into her own face in the oval glass opposite her, the stage-side the box, see how handsome she is, yet not be happy. She suddenly turns her head, for the box-door opens and the five voices exclaim :

"The young Rinaldo!" And then in mingled discord, "How are you, youngster ? How's the fair-haired Raphael ? All right, old boy ? Handsome as ever ? The bonnie wee thing !"

" Be quiet with you all, you ill-behaved boys.

I'll turn you all out :" and you have discovered that Lettice Tallington has one charm more—a voice! A voice that titillates : at least where natures are sufficiently sensitive to the influence of the most delicate but significant of instruments. It goes on : "I will, indeed, if you don't let him come to me. Reginald! Reginald! don't you hear? Come to me."

"Confound these fellows!" good-humouredly : "I can scarcely pass them. That's all right. How is Lettice? At least she is beautiful."

She touched him with her fan.

"You must learn not to say stupid things, child. I don't tell you you're handsome, though I know you are, and you know it too. Will you remember?

"Very well. What shall I say? I come to see you, and you scold me. See!" pulling off his glove : "been painting all day—sick to death of it."

"Who sat?" asked one of the party with a laugh.

"Your friend Lizzie, Master Morley. Jealous?"

"Confound your impudence. You've been sketching wicker baskets, crowbars, and step-ladders. I know your old governor won't let you do anything else yet."

"Leave him, Reginald. I tell you I want you to talk to me. Tell me about this opera. You don't know. Well, the story so far is— ha! they begin again. I should like silence, for I want to listen. They who prefer talking may go elsewhere. Attend, Reginald, and tell me what you think."

He did attend, at first, and it would have seemed as much at least from his own inclination, as from obedience to her behest. Clearly he had " music in his soul," but no less clear was it that the " lust of the flesh " was strong in that handsome boy, for the large blue eyes went wandering along at last the tiers, the boldest flights of song and most pathetic cadences despite. Handsome boy, indeed, he was, handsome in the privileges of eighteen. Not even down on those clear healthful cheeks, on that Sybarite lip, on that smooth selfish chin, not a freckle, not a hurtful speck on the

complexion throughout. And a flood of happy
sunlight seemed to be flung over his whole face
from the long golden waves of hair, fine even
in its redundancy. What his form lost by
want of height, was redeemed by its singular
slimness and negligently graceful motions ; and
looking on him, I think you might be pardoned
even by the most severe, if you conjured up the
similitude of a stem of corn, ripe and rocking.

The second act is over : Lady Harbledown
looks not well pleased, and renews her complaints. Suddenly, a hasty knocking ! "Box
H!" The sound of keys—the turning of the
lock, and Lady Harbledown has risen, displeasure
all departed, has stepped forward, and warmly
greets the at length arrived visitant.

"At last, Cyril! How are you? So glad
to see you, my dear boy. But why are you so
late ? "

"My dear Lady Harbledown, I could not
avoid it. I have grown industrious. I have
only just come from the House of Commons."

" What were you doing there ? "

" Reporting." He felt that he blushed.

"Learning shorthand. I am only practising, but I shall soon be perfect."

"What new fancy is this? Have you given up your studies for the bar?"

"It is no fancy," the blush breaking into a well-assumed laugh : "'tis a stern fact. I am learning it in order to be able to report your husband's speeches and get paid for it. But I am also studying to be a barrister."

"They must be queer people who will pay you for reporting Sir Wilfrid's speeches : even I never read them. You strange boy! But tell me—let us leave your—your shorthand—what have you been doing? Let me look at you. You are taller; you are handsomer; yes, sir, you are : but," and she sighed, "you are older!"

"Older! Am I gray? Am I palsied? Am I crooked? I am older; so are you; but you are—what you were."

"You used to be intelligent : I think it is the first time you have misunderstood. Again I say, you are older. I left you a boy; a boy, with a boy's privileges : I come back and find you nearly a man; a man, with a man's restrictions. Cyril will have to be Mr. Vavasour."

" Has a man no privileges ? "

" None that I wish you to possess—at least in my regard. I must look out for another boy to scold and spoil."

" I will be scolded still, and spoiled, too, if I may. What shall I do ? Shall I ruthlessly destroy this promising growth ? " And he played with his well cared-for whiskers.

" You know you would not for all the women around us, you vain boy. But—what manners. I forgot to introduce you to—your oldest friend."

Vavasour turned hastily.

" Stephen ! "

" Yes, old fellow, Stephen. No other. I should not have known you a bit, though Lady Harbledown prepared me. How long is it ? Three—four—nearly five years, isn't it, since we saw each other ? "

" Yes, yes. Five, this summer. Have you joined your regiment ? I saw you were gazetted; but I thought you were in Germany."

"Oh! I have lolled about in innumerable places since."

"Really, this won't do," broke in her lady-ship. "I merely wished to allow you to recognise each other, but I did not intend you to rush into each others' arms in this manner. I see you are both getting interested, and so I had better interfere at once. Suppose you go, Mr. Grafton, and pay your respects—where you will, till the next act. Otherwise this boy here will take no notice of me."

"By all means. I go."

"You'll come back, Stephen?"

"Of course he will, sir, but on my account, not yours. Well, I went to Nice."

"And elsewhere, surely?"

"I tell you, I went to Nice." And she looked at him with a questioning face. Vavasour persisted in the silence of a stare.

"And I looked for a name that used to be on your tongue pretty often, sir, but which you seem to have forgotten. I did not see a lovely face the whole time I was there."

"Then be sure you did not see hers. Humph!"

"Indeed! Where did you learn that grunt of levity? We used to have sighs, and starts, and bursts of eloquence and rhapsody. And Frailty's name is Woman, is it? I think we must have a new christening. So you have forgotten her?"

"Forgotten her! No, your ladyship—not forgotten, but she has gone—she has chosen to go; and I cannot follow."

"Would you, if you could?"

"I will not be questioned. How is Sir Wilfrid?"

"He is asleep—in the House of Commons somewhere. Why do you ask such stupid questions? If mine are more inquisitive, they are more entertaining. How did you spend your Long Vacation? Did you visit Dormer, the artist?"

"Yes; his son has come to town—is studying here. May I bring him to see you? He is such a handsome lad."

"You know you may bring him. But he has sisters. Are *they* handsome?"

c

" He has a sister, and she is "———

" Is what? Now, you know of old 'tis no use trying to deceive *me*. She is—what? "

" She is like other people ; exactly what lookers-on choose to fancy."

" You have improved in your fencing. But, pray, when did this reporting madness come upon you ? "

" Oh, some time in the autumn."

" When you were on your visit to Mr. Dormer ? Or immediately afterwards ? Can you make much by it ? "

Vavasour was deep in blushes again.

"Well, I will spare you to-night; but we must have it all out at Vernon Deep. When will you come down ? "

" I shall stay away altogether," he answered, with a merry air and a shrug of the shoulders. "I will not have my secrets wrung from me."

" Come on Saturday—I will meet you at the station ; and bring young Dormer with you. I shall learn much from him ; brothers have always plenty to say against their sisters."

" If I bring him down you must ask him

nothing. He is under my charge, and I must not lose my dignity in his eyes. Remember— you have said so—I have lived to have the privileges of a man."

"The restrictions, I said. Then you must not come to Vernon Deep."

"Yes ; I will."

"Then, come ; and play your boy's part still. Mr. Grafton returns. And see—the curtain rises. You had better sit there," pointing to the seat opposite her.

Just as Vavasour took the seat suggested, and the curtain rose on the last act, the handsome lad in Lettice Tallington's box, hastily, and without apparent reason, rose from his, and screened himself behind the girl's chair. Morley took the vacated position.

"By Jove! there's Vavasour ; and with Lady Harbledown, as of old. I have not seen her before, this year."

The exquisites behind came forward, and raised their lorgnettes in the described direction.

"What a lucky dog that Vavasour is," said one of them, "to be so much with such a splendid woman; and no one ever abuses either of them for it. His introduction to her was the funniest thing I ever saw."

"Yes; I've heard him tell it," said Morley. "Just like one of his mad tricks."

"Oh! I saw it all," said the other; "it was done admirably."

"What was it?" asked Lettice, who was leaning out of the box for the purpose of 'taking in' this so much lauded wonder of her sex. "What was it?"

"Simply this. It was at a hop in Hereford Street—some people I know. One of her numerous admirers was begging her to dance with him, and she excused herself. Then, said the fellow, 'Of course, you can't dance with anyone else to-night.' 'Oh, yes! I will,' she answered, in her way. 'I will dance with Captain Scott,' and she turned to him. Scott of the 11th, an awful muff, who dared not have asked Lady Harbledown to dance with him to get his majority. What did the fool do, but as soon as she said (of course she did not mean it) that she would dance with him, than Scott

coloured up, trembled, and blurted out—'Um
—er—I'm very sorry, but I'm engaged for
the next dance.' Vavasour was standing close
by—had never seen Lady Harbledown before,
but had overheard this conversation, and caught
her eye just as Scott stammered out his ridiculous excuse. 'I am not engaged,' he said,
maliciously; 'and I will dance with Lady
Harbledown.' 'I have not even the honour of
knowing your name,' she answered aloud, with
a malice and humour she is so proud of. We
all stared, for none of us knew Vavasour—a
mere boy, but a devilish good-looking one. We
stared a good deal more, I can tell you, when
he said, with a most self-possessed smile, 'If
your ladyship will wait one moment, I will seek
some one who will come back with me and tell
it to your ladyship;' and still more, when,
without more ado, she stepped forward, took
his arm, and waived the introduction. And she
has petted him ever since. I think Sir Wilfrid
likes it rather."

"Who is Sir Wilfrid?"

"Her husband."

"Oh! Do you know him, Reginald?"

"Know whom?"

"This Vavasour they're speaking of."

"Know him? rather. Morley and I were at school with him."

Lettice, by a quick eye and an interested one, might have been seen ever and anon looking in the direction of Lady Harbledown's box: Lettice, who rarely emerged from behind that yellow damask curtain, and used the lorgnettes so sparingly. I suppose she had her reason.

Carriages are stopping the way; linkmen are shouting; girls are pettishly cross with their brothers, but admirably patient with their lovers, particularly with those who have not yet proposed. A stranger would have wondered how all those people would ever find their carriages and get home.

"I *must* go, Lettice—indeed I must. No! I cannot see you to your carriage. I must go; good-bye."

"You are very unkind, Reginald! and very ungrateful. Go then. Frank! Lord Alender! Give me your arm. Thanks!" (*sotto voce,*

"What does the child mean?") "Morley, what is Vavasour's name?"

"Vavasour!"

"Mrs. Tallington's carriage stops the way!"

"No—no—Christian name?"

"Oh—er—Cyril."

"No, Frank! no; I go home alone."

"See, Cyril! quick. Getting into her carriage; long white mohair cloak — no headdress. Stupid boy! it's too late—she has gone. Only, a—well, never mind."

"Didn't see her at all—was busy looking at you. Good-bye. Saturday, then?"

"Yes—and your young *protégé*."

"Well, Mabel, how is young Vavasour? Did he make his appearance?"

"Yes; and I have asked him to come down to Vernon Deep, and bring a friend of his with him. Did I do right, Wilfrid?"

"Oh yes! I'm always glad to see him, you know. He's a clever, gentlemanly boy, and talks Tory politics. And then, I know he amuses you, Mabel—a difficult thing to do."

She laughed briefly.

" What have you been doing at the House ? "

" Oh, a wretched Beer Bill—awfully slow.   I think debates grow stupider and stupider every night."   And Sir Wilfrid Harbledown proved his rights to be critical upon stupid people, by flinging himself into an arm-chair and relapsing into silence and a cigar.

Not a word — no, not a look, not a glance of pleasant praise for that exquisite presence of hers! Not a syllable— not a hint of appre-ciation of that perfect toilet—daringly original, even in its most serene and classic art !   No gentle hand upon the glossy hair ; no enfolding arm around the tempting form ; no caressing voice ; no fond questioning to that woman's soul, with all its marvellous capacities of reply. We do not all of us prefer Beer Bills, Sir Wilfrid, even when they are stupid, to operas when they are new, and fair women ask to hear them.   There *are* men who indulge neither in brutal silence nor the insulting solace of a cheroot.   O fool, fool ! other hands may love to rest where they should not ; other lips can

utter winsome flatteries when they should preserve a decent reticence ; and eyes there are
with strange talent for looking delicate approval
of silken folds, and of charms the more suggested by the signal skill with which they are
concealed. Though a husband forget the offices
of a lover, a wife generally remembers the privileges of a woman ; and marriage, as well as
property, has its duties no less than it has its
rights. Does it cost much to praise a glove ?
to approve a fan ? to enquire about a skirt ? to
suggest an alteration in a head-dress ? to seem
to steal admiration of a well-enclosed foot ? It
is cruel—I say it is savage—to deny homage
such as this. Why, I told my dear mother
yesterday—my mother with her widow's weeds,
and her snow-white hair—that she looked "so
nice," and I vow I made her as happy by those
two simple words as if I had dragged her youth
out of the grave, and arrayed her in the orange-
blossoms of her wedding-morn. Women will
pardon you your hatred, and will pass acts of
oblivion upon your ill-judged injuries ; but—
and they are right—they will never forgive you

for the intolerable insult of your unmanly indifference!

A summons delivered in the shape of sundry kicks at his outer door made Vavasour fling on the coat he had but just doffed, and seek, with some haste, the excuse of so unceremonious a visitor.

"Who can want me at this unearthly hour? Pest on the door!—that's it. Why, Reginald! what brings you here this time of night?"

"Oh, nothing. Only I'm dead tired. I saw the light in your window, and"——

"You ought to be in bed." Looking at his evening dress. "Where have you been?"

"To the—the theatre with—er—Morley."

"You are always going to the theatre with Morley. You have no right to go to the theatre with him or with anybody as often as you do —throwing away the money of which you have so little, and for which others work."

"It cost me nothing. Morley paid for it."

"You ought to be ashamed to let Morley pay for you as he does. I never saw a fellow with so little self-respect : I verily believe you would accept a favour—even if it were money—from a stranger in the street."

"Don't be cross, Cyril! I'm so done up. And"——

"I have not the slightest doubt you are done up—it would be wonderful if you were not. If you did choose, as you always choose, to go to the theatre at Morley's expense, you might have had the sense to go home after it. It's now a quarter to two. You have not only been to the theatre, but you've been to some disreputable hole, and"——

"I have only been to Evans's."

"Well, if you won't sleep yourself, *I* want to sleep ; and therefore the sooner you go, the better."

"*Do* let me stay here in the Temple, to-night —I'm so fagged! Do, Cyril! like a kind fellow."

"Stay here ? nonsense. Why, it is·but a mile to your lodgings. Really, this is intolerable—I will not be knocked up in this way. Now—good night."

"*Do* let me stay, old fellow! I can sleep quite well in the arm-chair."

"It's no use : I won't "——

"Well, I can't go home—that's certain ; " blurted out the handsome lad with desperate frankness.

"And, pray, why not ? "

"Because—because "—and then rapidly— "because I haven't paid for my lodgings for three weeks, and *can't* pay for 'em, that's the truth."

"Where is the money I got you for those sketches ? "

"You know I went to the Derby."

"I know I asked you to go with me : I offered to take you. But that was too quiet for you, and you must needs go in Morley's drag, with a set of spendthrift disreputables, who have however at least this advantage over you—that they are not amusing themselves (or disgracing themselves, for anything I know), at the price of a parent's labour or the expense of a sister's self-sacrifice."

The concluding words were uttered with a

bitterness of contempt and accompanied with a stare of concentrated scorn that most men —grown, hardened men—would either have repelled or crouched beneath them. That fair-haired, smooth-faced boy did nor one nor the other. Had Vavasour been sufficiently cool or sufficiently indifferent, he might perhaps have seen that the young culprit was only rejoicing in the mistake of his hot arraigner, who, in accusing him of one baseness, was overlooking the existence of another, and a worse. Suddenly, though, in the silence that ensued, Vavasour's memory came back to him.

" A lie ! Reginald ! " A slight change in the colour now. " How dare you come and ask for shelter here with a falsehood as your excuse? Why, I did not give you the money till three or four days after the Derby."

" I know you didn't. The fact is, (it's no use trying to hide it,) I spent it this very day, like a fool as I am. I know you'll be savage, but I can't help it."

And with a pathetic levity, made up of ludicrous penitence for its stupidity and of

humorous indifference to its moral obliquity, the
boy went on to explain to Vavasour the proceeding by which he had that day chucked
away nearly five pounds. Hang it! he was
very sorry, and it was very wrong, and that
sort of thing—but they were such devilish
—such *very*, he meaned to say—such very
handsome girls, and it was so brutally wet,
and altogether—he could not help offering
them his umbrella; and then they were so
civil to him for *his* civility—he did not know
how it was exactly, but he found himself in a
shop with them, and giving his opinion about
their purchases, and offering to pay, and being
allowed to do so; and, hang it! if they didn't
get into a cab, and say they were going home,
and leave him standing in the street, hearing
their very laughter (at him, of course—he
knew that well enough) as they drove away.
And that was the whole story : and now Cyril
might be as savage as he liked. The thing
was done, and he couldn't help it : but mightn't
he sleep in the Temple, that night, at any rate ?

Very, very quietly Cyril answered him.

"I am not going to sleep here to-night : you can have my bed. I shall be here in the morning."

He went and slept hard by in a not over-comfortable chamber. A girl is asleep in quiet Onchester : far away, is it not ? Far away. But from her slumber, and athwart the distance, she claims gentleness for the boy-brother. "You will be kind to Reginald," had been the last words of a memorable visit. He had promised her with his eyes ; and he kept his faith.

"Please, Miss Lettice," a handmaiden was saying, much about the same hour of the night, as she passed and repassed the comb through her mistress's long streaming hair, "do tell me all about it again."

"But, Bertha, I have told it you a score of times."

"But are you sure, miss, that it was he ? "

"Sure ? How absurd of you ! I don't easily forget faces ; and I am not likely soon to forget his. He is very much altered ; but it was certainly Cyril Vavasour that I saw to-night."

And only too glad to comply with Bertha's
request, she began telling a story which, sure
enough, she had told her over and over again.
And since she related it more for her own
gratification than for her maid's instruction, it
is not to be wondered at if the relation was
rather straggling. I therefore will condense
her story and tell it in less meandering language.

CHAPTER II.

ONE October evening, seven years ago, when Cyril Vavasour, then a boy of sixteen, was sitting with his father and elder brother, Philip, over filberts and port wine, he solemnly announced to them his desire to publish a poem.

Had the boy announced that he had a very strong hankering after the moon, or for five hundred thousand pounds, Mr. Vavasour, being by nature both a practical and a dispassionate man, might in the latter instance have sent Philip for his banker's book, and shown his younger son that he did not possess, and therefore could not bestow, the wealth so unreasonably demanded ; and, in the former instance, have himself gone to the library, taken down the then popular treatise upon astronomy, and proved that the extreme distance of our nightly

D

visitant prevented all possibility of the yearning youngster's wishes ever being gratified. But how reason with a lad who assured you that he had written poetry, and wanted to publish it? Even Philip, the stolid Philip, put down the nut-crackers, and burst into spontaneous laughter.

It must not be supposed that Mr. Vavasour could not and did not appreciate poetry. Far otherwise. He knew by heart—he often quoted, and with the justest emphasis—Goldsmith's "Deserted Village," or Pope's "Essay on Man:" books so dissimilar as to prove that his taste was as liberal as it was correct. Cyril distinctly remembered nine years back hearing him read to Mrs. Vavasour the first canto of Scott's "Lady of the Lake," and could, he thought, trace his own initiation into the delight of verse to that very recitation. Nay, more, Mr. Vava-sour had—and would not have denied that he had—written in his youth what, like most of us, he thought at the time very tolerable rhyme. In his courtship of Cyril's mother, his brain had been unusually prolific in metrical assurances. But as for publishing such rubbish—any such

notion had never entered his head. Having
read poetry, and having enjoyed it, he was of
course aware that somebody in flesh and blood
had written it, and that the existence of verse
proved the existence of verse-makers. But
that his son should be one of them—that
anybody with whom he had the most fragile
acquaintance—anybody whom he had ever happened to brush by in the streets—should be
one of them, this had surely never occurred
to him ; as how should it ? Poets ! Why, they
lived in garrets, or in sponging-houses, had
quarrels with their landlady about the rent ;
if they got money, spent it in sherry ; never
had credit anywhere except with their publisher,
who had a mortgage upon them, and with
Posterity, when they had died of crusts too
eagerly partaken of, after long fast ; lived in
Drury Lane—Pope said so, and ought to know ;
sometimes got 60*l*. per annum for gauging beer :
and that sort of thing. What did the boy
mean ? Was he honestly in earnest ? Did
this poetry really exist on paper ? Or was it a
vaporous fiction, arising in some unimaginable

manner? Let him bring it down. Mr. Vavasour would like to have ocular demonstration.
Cyril went.

He returned with a rather formidable pile of
papers, which he placed upon the table, looking
the while more foolish than poets who are to
take the world by storm ever ought to look.
Mr. Vavasour by no means offered to read even
one sheet of this closely-written matter, but
sat staring at it as though he was not yet
perfectly justified in believing his eyes. Yes,
there it was, doubtless : stuff, each line of which
began with a capital letter. And such capital
letters! Most of it had been written out with
such fastidious neatness that there could be no
mistake about the destiny which its composer
intended for it. That was evidently not the
result of leisure hours; not even the offspring
of an ambition which limits itself to "private
circulation" only. That was—doubt it not—to
amaze the town! Philip, having gratified his
cynical curiosity, returned composedly to his
nut-crackers. Cyril had nothing further to say,
so stood silent ; though he had more than once

rehearsed what he *would* say when he made to his father the announcement which had been hurried on rather prematurely this evening, and had gone over in his own mind, and for his own benefit, the delight with which his father would receive the proofs of his earnest labour, and the results of his honest ambition.

In that stern face, every moment, too, becoming sterner, he could trace, it must be owned, no symptoms of delight : self-flattery could not delude to such an extent as that. But I think he little guessed what were the exact interior workings of Mr. Vavasour's mind, which threw so unpleasant a shadow upon the usually cheerful countenance. The fact was, that Cyril's conduct had been, on various occasions lately, of such a kind as to cause his father—justly or unjustly—uneasy misgivings about how he was likely, as the phrase is, to turn out. He was altogether dissatisfied with the boy. He was, in his way, as fond of this younger son as, I believe, was ever father yet. Truth to tell, he was rather proud of him ; nowise underrated his abilities, as far as they had been manifested,

and acknowledged in him the presence of kindly
generous impulses, such as favourably influence
the least affectionate dispositions, of which Mr.
Vavasour's assuredly was not. But, all this
granted and allowed for, there remained much
to mar the satisfaction of the Present, and
to render it a duty to anticipate the Future.
Neither the boy's fits of silence, which were both
frequent and protracted, nor his outbursts of
enthusiasm which, though less common and less
lasting, were even more remarkable and more
significant, afforded his parent excessive comfort.   Essentially of a philanthropic and genial
temperament, it plagued, it annoyed him to see
any one, how much more one of his own family,
in moods which, if they did not betray positive unhappiness, argued at least the absence
of ordinarily good spirits.   He could not bear,
as he said, to see people "mope," and Cyril
moped.   When these fits left him, they would
be succeeded by extravagant loquacity in which
sparkled, doubtless, a wit—sometimes, but rarely,
a sarcasm— inconsonant with his age ; but more
frequently and more prominently,what appeared

a wild, fantastic, visionary chivalry that, but for the language in which it was advanced, would have suited, Mr. Vavasour thought, a boy of twelve rather than one of sixteen. And then there was about him a stupid sensitiveness—a gift of tears, (a fatal one, surely,) coming no farther than the eyes, but apparently as far back as from the heart ; and joined to this were occasional marvellous explosions of the sternest self-will, and a scornful irascibility, which, though evidently at issue with the lad's chief bent, got a-top sometimes, and played, it appeared to ordinary spectators, some very peculiar antics. All these eccentricities—for such he regarded them—had puzzled Mr. Vavasour considerably. *Now*, they ceased to puzzle him : *now*, he had the clue to the illogical labyrinth of the lad's character. A boy who could write poetry and want to publish it, could be expected to go through a great many other almost equally wonderful performances. And did not this poetry, this infernal poetry, explain his whole conduct ? Mope ! He might well mope. It would have been very strange if he had not

moped.   Then these odd, out-of-the-way views,
and impossible manias—were they not either
the cause or the result of this rhyming disease,
or both ?   And the self-will ?   And the stub-
bornness ?   And the outbursts of magnificent
anger ?   A boy who went about in a dream,
in a fool's paradise, when woke up by the
admonitions of the actual world, was sure to
exhibit all three.   The puzzle was unravelled;
the boy was a mystery no more.

So thought the man of business, as he sat
eyeing that wonderful waste of valuable paper.
But his thoughts did not halt there.   Cyril had
fallen into the fatallest error : Cyril from such
must be rescued.   He must be disabused of his
absurd fancies; must be shown that the track
upon which he now was, led absolutely nowhere,
or if it led anywhere, led to very queer places :
to Maiden Lane, to Grub Street, the King's
Prison, to the open air in St. James's Square,
and other such desirable places of entertainment.

The disease must be attacked at once.   Once
and for all, Cyril Vavasour and Poetry must

part company. He was usually, when his father manifested conviction, passively submissive; and when most offended, never sulked. Mr. Vavasour little doubted but submission would result now.

"You must promise me, Cyril, to abandon this idle habit, and to write no more verses. When I say 'idle,' I don't mean that *you* are idle ; but the occupation is an idle, a useless one ; nay, worse than useless—it is extremely pernicious. Two classes of people are justified in devoting themselves to it. Firstly, they who have no objection to starving ; secondly, they who, from their wealth, are never likely to starve. I believe you are sensible enough to appreciate the disadvantage of hunger ; and if not already aware, become so now, that when your education is over, you will have to make your own way in the world. The very best result that could come of your publishing that stuff there, would be that you would only make a fool of yourself, which I am sure you have no desire to do. Your word will be quite sufficient for me : promise me you will write no verses beyond what your school-duties impose. Promise me, you hear, Cyril!"

"Cyril!" echoed Philip. "My father speaks to you; don't you hear?"

Yes, Cyril heard well enough. And Cyril will say something, when he can find the words he wants; but he is not quite so ready or so eloquent as usual. When the words do come, they are neither very numerous, nor very uncommon.

"I—I—can—cannot promise, sir!"

"But you must. I require—I insist upon it. This sort of thing I will not have. It makes you stupid—melancholy—irritable: and will, if persisted in, unfit you for serious work, when serious work comes, as it must soon. Be led. Once more, promise me."

"I am very sorry, sir; but—but I cannot. It is—is impossible."

"Impossible! What on earth do you mean? Impossible? Impossible to give up writing that nonsense? What is there impossible in it? You have only to will it."

"But I do not—I cannot will it."

"Then, sir, do you mean to refuse to promise me? In plain words, do you intend to continue this comedy of spoiling good paper? Frankly, now, I will not permit it. For your sake I act; for yours only. If you cannot take care of yourself—of your interests—I must do so for you. *I* will be no party to this foolery. Once more I put it to you. Promise me to *try* to abandon this habit, and let us say no more about it."

"I will not—I could not deceive you. You know it, sir. In all else I will obey you. But what you ask I cannot do. I cannot even try. For three or four years" — (think of three or four years to a boy of sixteen! It had a sound and sense of forty centuries about it,) "for three or four years it has been "——

"Enough of this nonsense. I ask you to do a thing, and you refuse. Now, I will *see* that it is done. And firstly, as for this "——

As he spoke, he took hold of the pile of papers with a motion that unmistakeably pronounced the fire to be their immediate destination. Cyril rushed hurriedly forward.

"Stop, sir! I pray you! Papa, papa! You must—you—I—I "——

" You promise ? "

" No! I have told you I cannot, and I cannot."

" Then into the fire these papers go."

Instantly Cyril's whole manner changed. All heat, all hesitation, all nervousness passed away. Like a young reproachful spectre, pale and motionless, he stood, gazing fixedly on his father.

" I am your son, sir. To what extent bound to obey you I know not exactly, at this minute; but the moment those papers touch the fire, that moment I leave this house."

Quietly, slowly, deliberately, Mr. Vavasour stirred the fire; separated the papers, and scattered them over the blaze, which lapped them with a savage thirst.

" Now, sir, I go."

Quietly, slowly, deliberately—even as his father had given his heart's treasure to the flames—Cyril turned towards the door; gently opened, gently closed it. Philip leaped up from his seat.

"Cyril! you little stupid!"

"Stay where you are, Philip!" came Mr. Varasour's voice from the hearth, in tones strangely harsh. As he spoke, they heard the hall-door close, and then no more.

A kind hand from outside pushed back the wooden grating, through which could be seen the horses in their stalls. The Arab slept. "Good-bye, old fellow!" said doubtfully, and with a sough as of suffocation in it; then the grating gently replaced. And the mother? The loving, ever-exculpating mother! No good-bye to her! No, indeed. *She* would not have let him go—rightly or wrongly, she had kept him; the young rebel knew that well enough. He looked up at her window, as he repassed the house from the stables, and murmured something. The very night-air, the still, listening, wakeful night-air even, did not catch it. Cyril! Cyril! As he strode on down the gravel-walk, the laurels caught him. Cyril! Stay, Cyril! Cyril! Why, the weeping willow bent lower, lower, and got tangled in his vagrant hair. Cyril! Cyril! Heed thee! heed thee!

Cyril! Mournfully—oh, how mournfully !—broke the November moon through the dense clouds that had all night hitherto dimmed her, and looked down—*came* down—to him. Stay! boy, stay! All rustle went the very naked Alwoodley branches, all together. Cyril! Cyril! haughty, selfish Cyril! . . . Onwards! the gate in view. Along the traversed distance, a neigh —a faint, trembling neigh—but Attila's! O Cyril! What! A hand upon the gate. It *will not* open. Again. A grating, creaking sound —a heaving of the dissonant hinges. A clang! and it is done. O Cyril! Cyril!

*   *   *   *   *

But what has all this to do with Lettice Tallington? Very much, indeed, if you will only be patient for a few lines more. Cyril had scornfully flung home behind him, and dashed into the thick of London, of which he knew absolutely nothing. He had, however, either the good sense or the good fortune to take small, cheap rooms in the north-west end of the metropolis, where he set himself to work to write out from memory the poem that had been so ruthlessly consumed. In the same house were lodging together two young girls, very little if any older than himself, one of whom was always spoken of by her landlady as Miss, and by her companion as Tiny, Forde. The house was small; and, constantly meeting each other on the staircase, they soon formed at least a speaking acquaintance. A very few days led Cyril into their sitting-room. He was the sheerest and most innocent child on earth; but he was very lonely, and not at all indifferent to a pretty face and soft manners. Tiny Forde had both, and, what he wanted still more just now, a sympathetic disposition. Nearly all young people are egotists, and Cyril was an egotist of the purest water. Would she care to know what he was doing in London? Yes, above all things. She had often wondered, but of course had not liked to question him. He told his story, and she certainly did not disappoint him on the score of interest. But he was not quite so gratified when Tiny unmistakeably manifested it as her opinion that he had been very foolish to leave home, and that the sooner he returned the better. Nothing could come of leaving home, she said very earnestly, but troubles, and sometimes worse. He could not but believe that she would be very sorry to lose his society, but, "Do go home again," she finished ; "do go home again."

He could not. *That* was quite out of the question. She did not know his plans, he would tell her. This same poem he had written again ; he had nearly finished. In a few days he would send it to a publisher. There was only the gap of a few weeks between him and Fame. He read her some passages, which she admired immensely ; and likely enough her admiration, though uncritical, was genuine. He went on working day by day, and day by day having fireside chats with his new acquaintance. The other girl seemed rather to avoid them when they were together, much to Cyril's comfort ; for he took almost as strong a distaste for her as fancy for her companion. And less and less, as the young would-be poet came and uttered eloquent rhapsodies about himself, did Tiny dwell and insist upon his returning home.

He had positively got somebody to believe in him.

But she was his first and last proselyte. Fortune does not always favour the brave, as many a fine fellow has found to his cost, and as Cyril after a few weeks found to his. Why should I make a long story of what everybody but himself, and such like boyish ignorant enthusiasts, could guess at once ? He spent no little time and underwent no slight mortification in visiting publisher after publisher, not one of whom would so much as look at his manuscript. At last he found a firm who would be happy to have the opinion of their reader upon it. Three weeks were consumed in waiting for this opinion ; a delay, however, which appeared to Cyril but commensurate with the importance of the matter. It was Christmas Eve when he received a letter which stated that the reader had reported favourably ; that there was more merit in the poem than in many recent works which the public had accepted ; and that the writer would be happy to see him on the subject of publication. Here was balm in Gilead !

The glee of the young people was immense. Tiny thought that he had better go at once. So off he went. Poor fellow! They thought very highly—very highly—of his poem, and would be most happy to *publish* it for him. The expense to *him* would be thirty pounds. Cyril was dumbfoundered, and stammered out as much.

"Indeed! Oh, yes; the author always publishes at his own risk, till—till he is known. That is always our plan."

"I am very, very sorry," stuttered Cyril; "but I—I—in fact, there is an end of it. Plainly, I haven't the money. I'm sorry to have troubled you, but"——

"Oh, no trouble. *We* are sorry you have had the trouble. I have a train to catch : you will excuse me. Shall we send your manuscript ?"

"No, thank you; I can take it."

Through the snow, now falling fast and thick —through the sloppy streets—through the long distance—Cyril travelled home : faster growing his pace—his head bent to the pitiless wind—

but minding not at all the flakes that gathered
in his long curly hair, settled in his unprotected
bosom, and turned his very feverish breath to
icicles. Tiny heard him come in, and rose to
meet him, and hear his tidings. But as she
reached the landing, she heard his own door
close upon him. She wondered he did not
come to her; it was scarcely kind, after all the
interest she had taken. Then she thought
that he had gone to take off his wet things
and would be with her directly; so she went
and sat down again. But no door opened.
Still longer she waited, wondering; still he
offered not to come. She trode gently down-
stairs; she stood beside his door. She listened:
no sound. She went back to her own room,
and again waited. Again she went gently
down; again stood by his door; again listened.
No sound. She knocked timidly. No answer.
She knocked again—more firmly. No answer.
Again: and, this time, loudly.

"Come in!"

She entered: she had never been there before.
He sat in front of the fire in an easy chair; its

back to the door and to her. He did not offer
to move. She walked across. As she reached
the hearth, she saw that the blaze of the fire
was completely smothered by a pile of half-
consumed paper. She put her hand gently on
his shoulder.

"Cyril!"

She had never yet called him anything but
Mr. Cyril; but she knew it was only his Christian name, though what the other was he had
never told her.

"What's that, Cyril?"—pointing to the fire.

"It's the poem, Tiny."

And sure enough, it was. With his own
hand, spontaneously, unurged, the son had come
to perform that very act of sacrifice for which,
when performed by the father, he had indignantly left that father, the fondest of mothers,
Philip, Attila, home, everything, behind.

Tiny, however, for the moment forgot all about
the poem and its melancholy history; for she
became alive to the state in which Cyril had
returned home, and this for the nonce engrossed
all her attention. She forthwith began wringing

his long, neglected curls, dripping as they were with the now thawed snow. She got his sponge and his towel, and did what she could there and then to make the best of it. To all of this he sat submissive, as though he should not care if she were to cut his whole hair off, or disfigure or ornament him in any way she thought proper. At last he made an effort, and tried to say—

"There, Tiny, that'll do; thanks."

"No; but it will not do. You must dry yourself well, and cheer up."

And within an hour of his return, they were sitting together upstairs, roasting chestnuts and being moderately merry. One would expect her to be falling back upon her old opinion, and urging him to return home; but on the contrary, she was casting about her to see how he might remain, and yet accomplish his purpose. She could not bear to lose him now.

"How foolish of you to burn it! But I suppose you can remember it all. You may yet want it. Can't you write prose as well as poetry?"

Cyril thought he could. He had done so at

school often enough, and his style had been the subject of much admiration.

"Could you not write a tale in prose, like the tales I showed you in the journals? They are very interesting, and everybody reads them ; and I know the tales are paid for, and you would be paid; and then you might save money to publish the poem yourself. Don't you see?"

Yes, Cyril did see, and brightened up proportionately. Was she sure those tales were paid for? Quite sure? Yes—quite. She could prove it by the "Notices to Correspondents." Well, now, suppose he wrote a tale for one of these. A short one, say, at first.

"It's all very well, Tiny; and it's very clever and very kind of you to suggest it, but it would take me some little time to write a tale, even a short one, supposing I could write one at all—and I dare say I could. But what's to be done in the meantime? The fact is"— and here the speaker blushed, and did not look quite comfortable—"the fact is I—I—have got to the end of my—my supplies"—and here he tried to laugh, but it was a poor effort. "They were not very large to begin with, and they are gone. You know I should have had more if I had been going back to school ; but it was the end of the holidays, and I had not got stocked again. I've sold my chain"——

"Oh, why did you do that, little goose ?" .

"How could I help it, Tiny ?"

"Very easily ; " and now *she* laughed, and her laugh was more natural than his.

"I don't see how. Then, there's my watch —all I've got left ; for I sold a pin, too, and I must sell the watch, and I don't like. You know—or you don't know—but mam—my mother gave it me ; and I don't like parting with it—but I must, for all that."

"Oh, no ! you needn't."

And Tiny went on to inform Cyril that he had a rich relation of whom he certainly had never heard before : a well-to-do uncle, that never dies, but has many nephews, all of whom he is ever ready to oblige on an emergency. Plainly, she explained how he might get money by his watch without parting with the full ownership ; and how he would be able to regain entire possession of it by repayment of the capital, when capital had become plentiful by the sale of these stories.

"I'm sure," she said, "I would not let you part with it at all, if I could help it; but I am —why, much as you are. I will always help you when I can."

Whereupon Cyril intimated, kindly enough, but peremptorily, that he had no idea of letting her or anyone assist him in that fashion. But he thanked her much for the information about the watch, and said he would rather obtain the necessary means through that method than by losing his mother's present altogether. Tiny would do it for him, did he not like going himself. Would she? He did not know how it was done. She might do *that*, if she would. So she did it : bringing him back eight sovereigns, and a piece of cardboard, which latter she told him he must by no means lose. And so it came to pass that the project of returning home, which on the first blush would have seemed the only practicable scheme left, was never discussed at all; but that Cyril was to live on his newly-acquired property, and meanwhile coin from his brain wealth-bringing tales. He worked awfully hard, wrote one tale and sent it off, and set to work at once to write another. The first had been acknowledged in the " Notices to Correspondents." The weeks passed on; Tiny thought it was time he should make some enquiry about it. He received for reply that the magazine had recently changed hands, that the editor had inherited a mass of manuscripts, among which Cyril's should be looked for and returned. This was rather a severe blow. Still, there was another journal, and Cyril had completed his second story, which was duly sent off. More delay, more enquiries, more weeks gone. Cyril grew poor and impatient. He wrote an importunate letter, begging for an immediate reply. He got one, saying that the proprietors of the journal could not pretend to return rejected communications.

That night Cyril passed in incoherent ravings, and Tiny in trying to make sense of his speeches and to allay the fever which was on him. The morning brought consciousness and something like sleep. Complete rest and a recumbent position were ordered. During this state of things Tiny nursed him with unsurpassable tenderness and the faithfullest assiduity ; leaving him seldom, and then for his wants, not for hers. And she seemed to have nothing in the way of remuneration, for the doctor had forbidden conversation ; so talk Tiny would not, despite the invalid's many provocations. Even when she bent over, bathing his hot dry face, she only smiled at him, commanding silence with her finger on her lips, when he moved as if to thank her for her care. Under such ministrations he was coming round, and the fifth day saw him sitting up. The fever once gone, he felt, he said, well enough ; he should like to go out; he was sure he could walk any distance ; he was quite strong; what the doctor said was all nonsense. Tiny, however, would be obeyed, confining him strictly to his room ; and now talked to him freely enough upon all topics but the fatal one which had induced this last lamentable state of things.

The week came to a close; the doctor pronounced him all but convalescent; the next day he might go out. He would give a new prescription—the last, but an important one, and he should like it to be made up at the Apothecaries' Hall. Tiny said it should be; she would go herself. The Apothecaries' Hall was at Blackfriars somewhere—a considerable way off; she should be away perhaps a couple of hours, so Cyril must not think her long.

She had not been gone a quarter of an hour when Cyril's attention was attracted by a noise proceeding from upstairs. The landlady and Miss Bolton were evidently engaged in an altercation, in which both were clearly out of temper. That, however, was no concern of his. But higher grew the pitch of the voices. Then he recognised Tiny's name—again—and again; then his own, most distinctly. Surely he was interested in this. He went upstairs. As he reached the landing the landlady brushed past him and descended, flushed and hurried. He entered, and found Miss Bolton in much the same condition.

" What is all this about ? " he asked. " I hear Tiny's name, and then I hear my own. So I concluded I had a right to inquire."

" Oh, it's only between the landlady and me. We cannot pay our rent this week."

" Who cannot ? "

" Miss Forde and I."

" But what has that to do with me ? Why should my name be introduced ? "

" Why, you see it's all Miss Forde's fault. She cannot pay her share, though *I* can ; and Mrs. Muster says it comes from waiting upon you. You take up all her time."

" How ? She used to be with me before ; at least, I with her."

" Yes, but only during the day."

It took many more words than we require here, to make the smooth-faced, innocent lad understand of her, who had been best and kindest friend to him on earth, what he knew but in the vaguest sort of way of people whom he fancied he had never seen ; passed though he must have scores of them in his wanderings, with his poems or his tales under his arm,

through the London streets. Slowly, he began
to comprehend; slowly, to feel all outlook of
hopefulness drifting from him; slowly, to stare
upwards and find no stars in heaven!

        ○   ○   ○   ○

Three hours after the sun had set, an iron
gate creaked on its heavy hinges in sullen
obedience to a hand whose weight it had not
felt for near five months. A quick but measured
step upon the broad, winding gravel-walk broke
upon the otherwise all-silent night. The trees
did not seem to know their visitant; the stars
seemed to care not about him or his purposes.
The laurels had no welcome; the weeping-
willow lent no salutation; no neigh came floating athwart the distance. The lad walked on.
He had reached the hall-door: through its glass
arches he could see the lamp hanging as of old,
he could see the library door on the right, half-
ajar, and that lights were within; and nothing
more. He put his hand on the handle of the
front-door; it opened to him. He went and
hung his hat on the stand, pushed the library
door gently back a little farther, and stood

within. On the sofa sat the son ; on the hearth, the father ; besides these, none.

"I have come back, sir. Am I welcome?"

"Welcome, if you have come to remain ; welcome, if you have returned convinced ; welcome, if you have returned cured ; welcome, if you are penitent."

"I have returned, sir—thus!"

"Then stay. Stay to show that you begin better to understand your position ; that you are not so inflated with self-esteem, or so led away by self-will. Your future conduct can prove all these. I hope it will do so. There is my hand, Cyril. Let us hear no more of it."

The hand was scarcely taken—the word scarcely said, when a quiet rustle and a quick step were heard in the hall, and the door again was pushed back. Cyril turned.

"Oh, my boy! my boy! Cyril! Cyril! my boy!" and then only inarticulate sobs, and bursts of woful joy, and many fondlings. She had him to her breast ; she was feeling his hair, his hands, his pale but feverish cheeks. Yes; it *was* her handsome boy come back—to go away no more. She had no reproaches for him; no taunts; no sermons, as yet, at least; only kisses, and tears, and overflowing tenderness, as if he had saved her heart, not nearly broken it; blaming him not that he had gone away, but loving and thanking him with her fond eyes and familiar touch that he had come to her again.

     ◇   ◇   ◇   ◇   ◇

By a bedside in London, all that night through, a girl knelt and wept. She had come home from her long Citywards journey, splashed and tired, but full of sustaining thoughts : for it was all done towards one for whom she cared, ah me! as such people will persist in caring. She had the medicine; the dear fellow would soon be all right again. She sought him at once, finding him not, however, but hurriedly writ lines, and a little golden heart, with a simple, "Wear it for the sake of what *has* been. And, O Tiny, Tiny, seek your mother, as I seek mine!"

"O Emma! how could you? how could you tell him? You knew—you must have

known that I loved him ; loved him only in all
this dreary world ! "

And so, the hours through, she knelt and
wept, with a gift or curse of tears surpassing
all but her sorrow. Oh, that *he* should have
known it ! He, from whom she had stowed it
away with such chaste care all along ! That he
should come to know what Tiny was ! After all
the weeks—after all the months—after all the
kind interchanges — the unwary passages of
guileless tenderness—all the day ministerings—
all the long night-watches—to end in this wise !

But Time, the great magician, has exorcised
all that sorrow. And if there be in the tone
of Lettice Tallington to-night anything that
recals the miserable break-down and suddenly
shattered hopes of the Tiny Forde of seven
years ago, it is not in any tear she sheds.

" Yes ; this is the little heart he left. I have
worn it ever since."

" Would you not like to see him again, speak
with him, talk it all over ? " asks Bertha.

" If he chose to seek me, yes ; not otherwise.
But I am sure my hair will do now."

CHAPTER III.

SIR WILFRID HARBLEDOWN had had the misfortune to be left by his father with an over-
pious mother, and ten thousand a-year. Against
either of these disadvantages singly he might
have struggled perhaps successfully, but both
united were too much for him. Had a thoroughly
worldly woman been his guardian when he
entered on his manhood, she would have turned
his income to good account ; had he inherited
nothing but poverty, a devout parent would
assuredly have much assisted him in enduring
his unhappy lot. But, as it happened, the young
baronet's mother only regarded his fortune as
an additional mundane temptation to her charge
against which it was her duty to oppose every
safeguard. She knew just enough of the

F

world's wickedness to be horrified by it; she knew just too little to be at all a judge how it was to be encountered. However, she had her views, right or wrong, and with the peculiar determination of one-ideaed people, she proceeded to enforce them. She was resolved that her son should undergo no unnecessary risks; and so she married him. She chose the time, she chose the maiden; and before he was twenty-two, Sir Wilfrid, innocent even of the mild inducements which a university career offers to ordinary passions and extraordinary possessions, found himself complimented upon a wife whose beauty was almost equal to her inexperience. Like him, she had never flitted through even a first London season. Mabel had fed Turkey poults, had cultivated prize fuchsias, and had never given her hand to anything more sentimental than the last-born calf. To say that the two young people did not love each other before they were married would be untrue, for did they not constantly meet and hold sweet intercourse under the watchful eye of Sir Wilfrid's mother? But to say that they loved from choice would surely be yet more untrue; for whom had the one or the other seen whom either was likely to prefer? The tall, elegant baronet was not likely to find a dangerous competitor in Tom the gardener, Dick the coachman, or Harry the groom. And to say the least, Mabel was *stellas inter Luna minores*—a very queen of the world among the dowager Lady Harbledown's dowdies of servant-maids; for even these had been chosen with a prudent caution against the possible irregularities of an over-tempted boyhood. Well, now they had "wooed and married and a'," where were they to live? At Vernon Deep wholly? So thought the timid mother, who had little idea of relinquishing her authority now that two instead of one were to be cared for—to be answered for before Heaven, were they not? But a man cannot come into a baronetcy and ten thousand a year, without the world knowing it; and the world usually considers that it ought, as well as mothers, to have some little to say to the destinies of one so very convenient to its purposes. It's all very well, said a section of it, for that pious old

woman (she would never have been called 'old'
if she had not been pious—she was scarcely
forty) to turn Harbledown into a builder of
churches and president of eclectic muffin-
meetings; but a fellow with his position
and his money owes something to his county.
The old baronet was a Tory, and such
must be his son. We are in low water just
now, and we can't afford to let all that stream
of wealth and influence run to waste. This was
the view of one section. Another appeared to
hold that it was an outrage upon the first
rights of society to withhold from its arena
such a pearl of all price as the beautiful, peerless
Mabel. We are sick to sleepiness, they said,
of all the old faces; we have not had an
accession to the ranks, Heaven knows when.
And here is a Venus Victrix, and her mother-
in-law is for keeping her down in that lumber-
room of Vernon Deep. Shall she, though? So
they talked. Nor is it to be denied that another
section—the bandit section—the section that
rides to the Derby on other men's drags, drinks
other men's wines, tampers with other men's

best treasures, gets bailed out by other men's money, and lives generally on a spendthrift succession of fools—complained most bitterly that its lawful prey was withheld from it by that religious old frump down in the country. Not a pigeon left, said these; not a single feather. Never was there such a time. Life is becoming intolerable—not worth the having. Not a single fellow now to give the long odds. One will have to pay for one's own dinner next. We'll see, though, if young Harbledown can't be brought to the scratch.

All these sections the dowager set herself to work to withstand most womanfully. How the battle between "the flesh, the world, and the devil," on the one side, and sermons, tea-meetings, and gothic architecture on the other, terminated, I am precluded from telling. For the various sections, who had nearly given up the game for lost, woke one morning, read their *Times*, and with many congratulations uttered one to another satirical R. I. P.'s over the deceased dowager Lady Harbledown. Sir Wilfrid at once took a mansion in town ; and his wife

was the belle and himself the "best fellow
going," of the ensuing season.

Five years ago was it since this had happened. Sir Wilfrid had got into Parliament.
The bandit section had had their way with him;
doubtless some other younger and now more
inexperienced and more squeezeable fool had
attracted them from him when he became (as
he did become) not over-responsive to their
exorbitant demands. They had not done him
very much damage in a financial point of view;
they had only made him just a little negligent
of his wife. This of course had improved the
opportunities of another section. But when I
say that it improved their *opportunities*, I have
told all. The country beauty had developed
into the town belle; the merrily-spoken girl of
the garden and the fields had blossomed into
the wit of the drawing-room and the *fête*. But
the goodness and the reputation which she had
brought to the city, she took away with her
whenever she left it. I doubt if any impertinence had ever been uttered or offered to her;
and of this I am sure, that even scandal had not

the courage to traduce her.   While others
seemed to think more, her husband seemed to
think less of her.   Perhaps he was not to blame.
Circumstance is very wayward.   Society had
cultivated in her the wit which he could not
appreciate, and the tastes which he knew not
how to indulge.   He did not find politics very
interesting, but he found his wife still less
so.

He had not been educated to the wants of
women, and after marriage this deficiency of
education cannot be supplied.   It is in trying to
make ourselves agreeable to women, and so to
win them, that we learn how they are pleased.
To acquire this, as all other knowledge, a
failure or two is necessary.   Sir Wilfrid had
never failed.   His wife had been won for him
by his mother, and now that she was his, and
there was nothing to gain, as far as he saw, by
studying her little desires, he very naturally
forbore from the study.   And the best that can
be said of him is that, had he been married to
a woman who would have treated him as some
will say he deserved to be, he would probably

have been very tolerant towards the infirmities of which he had been himself the cause.

When Cyril had first come across Lady Harbledown in the strange fashion which Frank Morley related to Lettice Tallington, the clever woman of the world conceived a signal liking for him. She had no children—she had no young thing about her. And here was a half-boy, half-man, whom ambition was driving on to manhood, but whose frank enthusiastic simplicity still held back almost to the impulses of a child. She, with her sober years (she was twenty-seven), might well be kind to the handsome, amiable, unpretending lad. Besides, she had discovered between them a relationship on her own side; a cousinship, such as most of us could find if so minded, but still a cousinship of which she made the most. Luckily Sir Wilfrid fancied him too, in his indifferent way; for Cyril could drink his wine and talk his politics quite cleverly enough to suit his host. And he was not sorry to find his wife affect one who was young enough for her to patronise and treat in half-mother's fashion, and yet able enough to amuse and be a welcome companion. So for his Conservatism Cyril got from Sir Wilfrid the best of port, and from Sir Wilfrid's lady, for his vivid egotism, the best of treatment and the kindliest, because the cheerfulest, of consolation.

With whatever formed intentions of concealment, Cyril had been compelled to revert to the original frankness of his first acquaintance with her sprightly, quick-witted ladyship. He had come down to Vernon Deep this morning (Saturday) as he had promised, bringing Reginald Dormer with him. And long before dinner-hour had he been obliged to describe how he was off with all old loves in order to be on with a new one. He might have almost spared himself the confession. She was an excellent judge of character, and she knew his through and through. When she had left England, he was raving about one Amy who had gone to Nice, and whom she was to be sure to find out there. On her return, he had no inquiries to make, was deeply interested in a boy not many years younger than himself, whose father he had been visiting, and was busy acquiring a knowledge of shorthand for the purpose of reporting. She put all these things together, and formed her conclusions.

He had such a dread of her humour, that he was not very eloquent in his self-defence, and could only say that he was young a year ago, and was old now, and that he never *could* change, &c., &c.

"My dear Cyril, I will side with you in the matter. Love whom you will, and as long as you will, only always come and tell me. If you don't, I shall find out, and then I *shall* be merciless. Nay, I am going to give you another chance. The Latimers have got back, and Blanche is sure to come in upon us this evening, and I will back my Blanche against your Mary. She is "——

"No, no, no; I care not what she is; it is not a question of beauty. All the beauties in Surrey are nothing to me. I have everything I want. I do not say that I have not seen handsomer girls. I do not say I have not seen cleverer girls—you see I am impartial"—(How proud

are young people when they think they can say
this with justice !)—"but she *is* good-looking—
at least to me. She is

> ' So wise in all she ought to know,
> So ignorant of all beside.'

And then, as I told you, she is very religious,
and a girl not pious is horrible. And I am
quite sure, when a man goes to heaven, 'tis his
wife gets him there. At any rate, it is *my* only
chance."

They were all sitting, dinner over, and the
flood of the warm June sunset coming on, on
the smooth straight lawn overlooked by the
long line of Tudor windows that have let in the
light of heaven on the home of the Harble-
downs for upwards of three centuries. The
additions and alterations of later years had
much impaired the original simplicity of its
architecture; but a provident destiny seemed
to have presided over it, even when submitted
to the essays of its most whimsical possessors;
so that even now, though certainly fantastical,
it could not be considered misshapen or even
altogether incongruous. Either its red brick

had been touched by the skilful hand of modern renovation, or it had strangely preserved its pristine brightness. Something of its freshness was doubtless due to the recently inserted plate-glass, which harmonises so well with the crimson virtue of the hard-baked clay. It was flanked on either side by trees, whose youth might perhaps have seen its foundations laid, so gnarled and knotted were their trunks, so many and so huge their ambitious branches. But in front, right away to the horizon, from the long waving grass in the meadow beyond the lawn, and separated from it but by an iron fence to where the Surrey hills gently sloping upwards touched and lost themselves in the evening sky, clear and untrammelled was the prospect. All between was verdure, meadows ripe and ready for the scythe, corn-fields as yet green and immature, and all thoughtless of the warm golden maidenhood to come, and the encircling sickle that would bear them away. Well might those boys—for nature never wastes her wealth when she proffers it to the young— well might they, though unaccustomed to sip their claret every day under the carved but massive oaken ceiling of Sir Wilfrid's dining-hall, declare that they would not be circumscribed by walls, and that they had not come down from town without intending to have the most of the summer sunsets and the Surrey air.

Of a sudden, from somewhere amidst the dense quiet foliage came upon them the sound —nearer—nearer—nearer—of a voice that had broken into song. A low, rich, yet tremulous voice—tremulous with the burden of its pathos —speaking a girl's soul. Nothing is so true a test of a woman's intelligence as the way in which she sings. Not the mere instrument, not the finished skill, not the well acquired art, proclaims her power; but that undiscovered something by which she grasps the meaning of the composer, and gives it adequate utterance. Nearer, nearer, nearer came the voice ; every note, every syllable distinct. Reginald held the crimson fruit suspended in his hand. Stephen woke even to a more satisfied appreciation of his position ; and, stolen from the landscape, Cyril's eyes turned in search for the spot whence came that harmonised and harmonising strain.

"Hush! It is Blanche; she does not know we are here."

Singing, she emerged from the trees, and stood full before them. A riding-habit of the simplest but strictest make, with not one careless crease throughout, enveloped but to display her form, and gave to her height perhaps even an additional grace; though they who had seen her in all costumes, averred that grace was what she never lacked. The suddenness of the interruption had also made her moment-arily pause in her advance towards them; and as Stephen (who knew her well), seeing her slight confusion, exclaimed, "You have stricken us into silence, Miss Latimer; but we applaud—we applaud now,"—she raised her hat, and let it fall along with her hand to her side, and moved her acknowledgments; a slight, very slight blush mounting from the smile of her parted lips, just heightening the exquisite bloom of those cheeks where youth and health held holiday, deepening the lustrous glamour of her hazel eyes, creeping up the long narrow brow, and then breaking against the nut-brown hair, and dying away like the last streaks of the sunset amongst the gloom of the distant hills.

"I had no idea you were so well surrounded; but I did think Sir Wilfrid would be here. He promised to be," she said, refusing the chairs offered her, and seating herself on the hassock at Lady Harbledown's feet, and taking her hand. "How unkind of you not to tell me you had guests. I have only just come from my ride. I dismounted at the little gate, and sent my horse home. But won't Sir Wilfrid be here?"

"Well, I scarcely know. He promised to come, as you say. What am I to do with these boys, if he does not; unless you will come to-morrow and help entertain them?"

"Then I hope my cousin will not come," said Stephen (he spoke of Sir Wilfrid); "better music, even sacred music, than politics and sport. But why may we not have both? What is there to prevent Wilfrid from being here ? No House on Saturday."

"But Sunday is a great day for private political dinners," Lady Harbledown remarked, (did she say it to excuse her husband ?) "He may be staying in town for one of them. Don't you envy him, Cyril ? I know you do. By the way, Blanche, you have been wanting to know clever, ambitious people. Yes, you have. She has been abusing the whole population of Surrey as *vauriens* and dull drones, and I know not what. Well, now, I cannot say—at least I must not say — that Mr. Vavasour is clever ; but he is as ambitious of climbing as—as— what, Stephen ? Help me."

"As a scarlet-runner or a chimney-sweep ; will that do ?"

Cyril laughed, but coloured, and might perhaps have been utterly at a loss, (not being willing, in the frank honesty of his youth, to repel a charge substantially so true, and yet not able to turn the charge to his own credit), had not Miss Latimer bravely rushed to the front.

"Let us laugh ; but there are many chimneys

in this world that want sweeping, and unless
some men have a climbing tendency, they will
never get swept.   And as for scarlet-runners,
I cultivate them, don't I, Mabel?   And I
have always noticed that the beautiful flowers
become more scarlet and more beautiful as they
mount."

"I am inclined to think, Miss Latimer," Cyril
answered gratefully, "that your flowers are
indebted both for their showy colours and their
progress upwards to your gentle and encouraging
care."   Then, with a happy laugh and skilful
turn.   "Without it, they would soon be as
unornamental and grovelling as—my dear
Stephen."

"You satirical wretch!   Won't I put on my
regimentals when I come down next?   I'm no
match for you in mufti, with that skilful tongue
of yours.   But only let me don my parade tog-
gery with the new shako, and then, Master Cyril,
I will give you ever so much start!   Why, you
know well enough, you shall write the best book
of the year, or figure at Westminster—isn't it?
—in the most important case.   Comes a young

G

jackanapes—that's not me, mind—in a red coat, and you and your favourable reviews, or you and your swell speeches, are nowhere."

"Will you keep your promise?" put in Blanche. "Try your theory. I declare, for my part, I like even your flippancy better than your frogged surtout, though neither is much to my liking."

"Cousin Mabel! Cousin Mabel to the rescue! or I surrender. Can we not rout them?"

"Ah, see there displayed what you would have us believe you do not possess! I will not help you; you need no assistance. Your cry to me is only the cry of the heart that longs for victory, even in a wit-combat. We all have the wish, though few the power. All would be victors, if they could. Every man is satirical in his heart; the favoured only with his tongue."

"Yes, yes; and we, Mabel, as well as they. Our ribbons are like their red coats or smooth speeches—small attempts at fame."

"Fame! fame! yes, I am for the fame that brings reward. The place nearest the fire in winter, farthest from it in spring; the seat near the prettiest girl, the first cup of coffee, the last cup of tea, the largest straw- berries, and the smallest Southdown ; in fact, the *pas* everywhere, and in everything ; these are rewards, and if fame will bring them, I am all for fame.   But I am pretty sure that all the fame in the world, if joined to an imprudent modesty or an indiscreet reticence, is a much longer and less certain road than the short and safe cut of a well-managed selfishness."

Such a speech was sure to be groaned down, and was the signal for a general rise.   Reginald attached himself to the new comer, and Stephen to his cigar.   Alone with Vavasour, the hostess was curious to know what he thought of her Blanche.

"What can I think ?   I am not, I fancy, one of those who have eyes and see not.   It is very good of you, encouraging such pretty faces at Vernon Deep.   I will come whenever you will ask me ; and when you don't, if your invitations slacken.   How is it one never hears of Miss Latimer ?   There is scarcely such another girl in London."

"Why, her papa is a singular old man; he takes her nowhere; and being without mother, and with the most selfish brothers you ever met, what can the child do? They have no house in town; I don't think they could afford it. Their place is very handsome; better, at least more luxurious, than ours; but Mr. Latimer must have sunk all or nearly all his money there. He was in business himself as a young man, though his father made the fortune. He soon gave it up, and has lived at the Grange ever since."

"But his daughter? Why has he educated her so well? She is singularly accomplished."

"Oh, with women that is a matter of accident. Really, I don't know where she was educated; but no doubt there were dozens of girls educated with her who cannot sing a note or conceive a remark. But he values her accomplishments just as much as her beauty: they are to him both accidents, which he would have liked to have avoided. Only the other day, when I was praising her to him, he said it would have been much better for her if she had been born with a hump."

" Old stupid ! "

" Yes, yes ; all very well for you boys. You like pretty faces and pretty dresses, would object to humps, and have not got to pay the bills. My Blanche is wonderful in her extravagances, even at that quiet place ; in town she would do her best to ruin him. Our country people notice them on account of her, and endure from him any amount of rudeness ; for he does not value or want their acquaintance, and shows them as much. Sir Wilfrid cannot bear him, and does not quite like my noticing his daughter ; though, like all of you, the face propitiates him. But he objects to the retired merchant, though he himself married the great grand-daughter of a barber, though he won't let me say so."

" What does he say of *me*, then ? " asked Cyril, slily.

" Never mind, sir, what he says of you. He is very kind to you, and so am I ; and you need ask no frivolous questions. I am not talking of

anything so slight as you, you egotistical boy.
We are talking of Blanche. Now, tell me, is
she not charming ? "

" Have I not already said so ? What
then ? "

" What then ! As always happens, to be
sure. Let us have no barren admiration. I
have started her against your last—or is it
already last but one ?—new fancy. You laugh ;
but you blush too. Listen to me. She will
have money ; not much, but five, six, perhaps
more, thousand pounds. Why are you pishing
and pshawing ? Of course you are to love
her ; and you are to set to work at once. Her
father—I will not compliment you—is not
ambitious for her ; and if he were, she would
laugh at his ambition, if it so suited her. I
fear they don't get on together very admirably.
He considers her vain and reckless ; she him
stingy and unreasonable ; and they are both
right."

" What an admirable wife ! What an admirable father-in-law ! Really, now, you *do* tempt
me. When shall I go in and win ? "

"I forbid sarcasm. Young people are allowed—are expected—to be conceited (and you, sir, quite fulfil the expectation); but they have no right to be satirical; it does not become them. I will not have my plans scoffed at. You are *not* to go in and win—you are to be patient. I want no more enthusiasm. I laugh when I hear of perfect beings—pious people—and shorthand-writing. You are only wasting your time. Attend to your profession solely, and—and—and marry—four, five years hence (she is but just nineteen) Blanche Latimer. That is my plan."

"I am becomingly grateful," said Cyril, gaily, raising his hat in mock acknowledgment; "but —but—I have *my* plan, too. I shall see *her* soon; when I leave town, you know. The Assizes will be on there; 'tis the circuit I shall go, and not far from Alwoodley—only some thirty miles. So I shall tell them at home I am going to see practice, and I shall see—her! Mahomet must go to the mountain."

"What an accomplished hypocrite! I think I must write to Alwoodley on the subject. It is so pleasant to have those things discussed in the family circle under one's ear!"

"Very! But my secret is my own—and yours; but yours only. I have not told any one—not even Stephen; and I should not have told you if you had not made me. Why should I? It is all a matter of feeling. I am not bound to advertise my sensations; and I could not bear to have them talked about. It is different from other things—it's so sacred—and she is so"——

"Oh, yes—yes!—certainly. Amy over again. I thought you had exhausted your superlatives in praising her; but I see you grow original. The singular part of love-passages is that they *all* are so different. Never was there anything like each one of them before. Ah! I know it all. So go to Onchester, and then come back to Vernon Deep. Blanche shall be there." So she bantered him in that kind way, all her own.

Philip Dormer had known but one romance in his whole life, but it had come in such a shape, and at such an age, that from its influence he had never escaped. He attained

twenty-one, and found himself, like Orlando,
"with poor a thousand crowns," and as nearly
alone in the world as a boy with a handsome
face, graceful manners, and avowed talents well
could be. His guardian, a strictly honest but
not very sensitive man, had regarded both the
charge of the lad and of the patrimony as a
burden; and was rejoiced when his *protégé*,
become his own master, declared his intention
of devoting what remained of his inheritance,
from the expenses of his education, to carrying
himself and his fortunes whither so many eager
believers in themselves had thronged before.
Dormer would go to Italy; he would wander
through the galleries of inspired canvas and
fresco, that have made its cities the studios of
the universe; would learn the secrets of their
success, and so foster, yet control, his own.
When you are travelling, you can get to know
pretty much whom you will. On the Continent
even English people are civil; and so you have
nothing but a knapsack, and be a gentleman in
your ways, Bloomsbury forgets to be inquisitive as to your crest. It was in Florence that

Dormer met the Chesterfields—father, mother,
two daughters, and a son much the same age as
himself. The acquaintance had commenced in
ordinary fashion enough at a *table d'hôte*, and
had ripened more romantically, at least so far as
the young people were concerned, in the galleries where the artist was at once an agreeable
and useful cicerone, a pleasant companion when
society was not plentiful, and when what little
there was, was not of the best. Mr. and Mrs.
Chesterfield, though country people of no signal
mark, were as self-important as though they
possessed a province, and had brought up their
children with no small appreciation of their
position. But, with some, love is stronger even
than instilled hauteur, and a heart is sometimes
lost even before the very winner becomes aware
that he has played for it. Yet, show me the
boy who wakes to know what he has won, and
will not exclaim, " The very prize I coveted."
And if that prize be a dark-haired, dark-eyed,
stately girl, and he have staked against her only
his eloquence and his conceit, I know well if he
will not fling his life's-love into the bargain, and

swear it was part of the original risk. One second—one throbbing, faltering second—Philip Dormer strangely stole from May Chesterfield her secret unawares ; and the next—throbbing —but no, not faltering—he was vowed her own, and she was plighted his, for all days thereafter.

This is an old story, say you. Very old ; and yet ever renewed. I will be pledged to say the same little performance is going on as I write or you read, in the same picture-gallery, in the same Florence, in this same monotonous whirligig of a world. Of course, then, there was a scene—a tremendous hurricane of taunts, threats, and tears ? Dormer was sent about his business and his painting ; poor May was lectured—scolded—bullied ; the whole family bustled back to England ; old Chesterfield never lost an opportunity of sneering at sign-painters ; and Miss Chesterfield is now Mrs. Captain Brown, and is famous for her anti-macassars ? Not at all. Not at all. It turned out quite otherwise, or I should not have troubled you to read or myself to narrate it. Dormer was quite

ready to listen to reason, or even to bend before
abuse. Five minutes before he had told May
Chesterfield that he loved her, it had never
struck him that she was more than the nicest
girl he had ever met (he had never met one
before) ; and five minutes after, though he loved
her much more than the moment when he had
so suddenly blurted out his newly-discovered
passion, he felt that he was a young fool, and
had only not done a dishonourable thing because
he had never intended to do anything at all.
Malice prepense at least he need not plead to.
But Love—young Love especially—is apt to be
very sanguine ; and he saw—they both saw—
how, in a couple of years, say, at the most,
Dormer would be celebrated, and be able to
lead his darling home ; and the parents meanwhile would patiently suffer an engagement,
whose limits were so very clearly defined. Who
has not annihilated time and space in this sum-
mary fashion himself! Thank God, we have
all been famous once for a quarter of an hour—
the quarter after stealing, like bungling imitators
of Prometheus, an evanescent fire from the

to-day heaven of a bonnibel's benignant lips.
Famous, indeed! Infamous, rather; at least,
so thought indignant papa and mamma. The
young jackanapes, to think of their daughter!
Who *was* the fellow? As for May, all girls
were alike, and were ready to take up with
Tom, Dick, or Harry, so any of those distinguished personages came in the guise of a pert,
soft-tongued troubadour. Dormer felt he had
made an egregious blunder, and was quite ready
to go away and be miserable for a month or two
—longer, if need were—for he felt fonder and
fonder of the impassioned young maiden. Now
comes the singular part of the history. Likely
enough—nay, there's not a doubt of it—you
will think what May did very unwomanly,
improper, monstrous, &c., &c. I am not going
to stop to argue it; only, she *did* it. The fact
is my affair; you may make the propriety yours
if you like. As Philip sat a-musing, that night of
receiving his dismissal from the hotel of his former
friends, a-musing and a-mourning, there came
to him a visitor. That visitor was May Chesterfield. He was carrying away her heart with

him, she said; would he leave herself behind?
He had owned that her love was his life, and he
was only dividing and destroying both through
devotedness to her and what he thought due to
honour and her parents' rights.   She knew
nothing of parents' rights.   She knew he loved
her; she knew she loved him—him only—him
wholly.   Her parents asked him to leave her;
her parents, to whom he owed nothing.   She
asked him to take her with him—she, to whom
he had promised all things.   Do you think them
poor arguments?   Be you in the same dilemma,
and be sure you will find them logical enough.
He *did* take her with him, and—they were
married: boy and girl, with £500, and the
whole world frowning on them, as it alone
knows how to frown.

Of course, he deserted her?   Or she, in a
couple of years, ran away with somebody else?
No, no, no.   I tell you this story is not like
other stories.   I know perfectly well—will grant
it you—that May deserved to be finally neglected
by the husband whom she had won against all
good breeding and the orthodox catechism of

courtship. I know perfectly well—will not deny it—that by all accepted canons, Philip ought to have been awoke some fine morning with a splendid pair of horns on his head, whatever that may mean. Very singular it may be, but very true it is, that these two young simpletons, who came to be married in this marvellous, monstrous manner, loved each other, I verily believe, more tenderly than ever pair loved yet; and discovered the strict necessity of one to the other to be so real and so complete that they positively held the scorn of the world as of no account, and the neglect of their relations as a misfortune patiently to be borne with, but not for a moment to be weighed against the consummate happiness of their mutual truth. Before a year was out, a little face laughed out at them from the cradle; and in time baby came to be called Mary. They were still in Italy. The wife believed in her husband's genius even more unswervingly than he, no great sceptic on the subject, believed in it himself; and she begged him to remain, and spend in that foreign land what was left of his narrow means, in becoming an accomplished adept in the art which was to win for him fame and fortune in their own. It was brave; it was successful. Three years went thus; and Mary's place in the cradle and in mamma's first thoughts was occupied by a frolicsome ever-crowing baby-boy, who was not yet called Reginald. Just enough money was left to carry them all home; but they took with them a picture. It was exhibited; and England held out her hand to another artist. Philip Dormer found himself at once with exactly the same moneyed fortune as on the strange evening when May Chesterfield had come to claim the fulfilment of his plight; but with opportunities of straightway increasing it to ten times the amount, should he accept orders thrust upon him with no little importunity. But he was by nature abhorrent of mediocrity; critical, and most so of his own attempts, when he went to Italy, he left it with a standard and conception of excellence attainable only by genuine inspiration superadded to the skill of acquired workmanship. The latter, once gained by, never deserts us; but we can no more command the presence of the other than we can God's sunlight or heaven's show of stars. It visits us but seldom; and he who strains at art when he is not inspired will soon cease to be inspired at all.

Dormer executed one order to enable him to settle himself and his much-loved charges at Ouchester. They lived quietly; but with every comfort that love finds requisite. It was the third year of his abode in England; the sixth of his sweet married life. He had finished his second picture, and was going to exhibit it the ensuing spring. It had been a long labour of love, made dearer still by his companion's encouragement and warm belief. She had ever been on his side—the side which leaned to slow, patient execution; had never hurried him, had never once asked him when the "Sermon on the Mount" would stand upon the easel, completed. It had been, it is true, somewhat delayed by his wife's being, during the whole winter, more or less out of health. At first, nothing was wrong, the doctor said; at first nothing ever is wrong. By March it was allowed that everything was wrong. Poor Dormer! He watched, he prayed, he wept, he vowed. To no purpose, all of it. She grew weaker, day after day; and the first primroses were on May Dormer's grave. She had told Philip, but an hour before she died, that at that very moment she was thanking Heaven for having been permitted to be united to him, and that she had never for an instant repented the choice of her early years. She had been allowed to remain with him but a very brief period; but God's will be done on earth as it is in heaven. She would have him refuse no opportunity of being reconciled to her family, though he had better not seek further what they seemed so resolved not to concede; but he must love the dear sweet pets, and his divine art, and work and wait patiently until they met again.

The Chesterfields had been all along inexorable. Dormer wrote to inform them of the sad event. None of them came to see May's tomb, Philip's tears, and the orphans' black dresses and wondering little faces. Mrs. Chesterfield wrote, giving her son-in-law to understand, in that circuitous language of scornful condolence which women alone can command, that he had killed her daughter, and broken her and her husband's heart : language rather hyperbolical if we consider the fact that, three months previously, they had indulged in merry-meetings and convivial *fêtes*, duly paraded in the provincial papers, on the occasion of their remaining daughter's marriage with a worn-out *roué*, who if he had nothing else left, had at least ten thousand a year, and the chance of a baronetcy.

The artist quietly read the letter, and quietly burned it ; and for the rest devoted himself simply to the strict fulfilment of poor May's last requests, loving his "dear pets" and his painting, now more even for her sake than for their own. His fame increased, but his grief did not lessen, with the growing years. His chief consolation some one, as we have seen, would give a good deal to take away from him. With the success or failure of the enterprise we are intimately concerned.

CHAPTER IV.

A NOT large, but, as far as slovenliness would permit, a luxurious apartment: every cushion soft, every chair easy. Not that ornament at all interfered. The rarest articles of virtù were cross-pipes, rattle-snake sticks, and rainbow smoking caps. The nearest approach to curiosities in the potter's art were German seltzer-water bottles; the mural decorations consisted of "Pas de Fascination," "L'Attente," nymphs " Aux bords de la Seine " " Aux bords du Néva," etcetera, bountifully displaying what I should think most men would go mad if their sisters did not scrupulously hide. To-night Morley held revel. These were his chambers in the Albany. His family lived down at Twicken-ham, and his father being an invalid, and his mother a fond wife, and somewhat of a devotee,

Frank was its only representative in town. He was supposed to be working in the bank of which Mr. Morley was, more or less, a sleeping partner ; but as nobody had discovered that he could be made very useful, and as everybody hoped he would follow in the slumbering wake of his father, he was allowed to follow his own bent ; and this inclined him more to betting-books than to banking ones, and led him oftener to Lord's than to Lombard Street. He was not a bad fellow, after all ; being rather an athlete, and having the double advantage of being a fool and knowing it. In all these he had the better of his guests, most of them having just enough wit to be impertinent, and just too little strength to enable them to be straightforward. Most of their faces were, like their conversation, à propos of nothing—mere blanks, like tomb-stones waiting for an epitaph, "Born such a day — died such another." There's our old friend, Lord Alender, whom we once saw at the Opera, and don't care if we never see again. His mouth is like the bung—his voice like the gurgle—of a beer-barrel ; his nose the exact portrait of the chipped stopper of a second-hand decanter. His eyes, with their struggling lashes, transmit as much light, and in fact resemble nothing so nearly, as the cobwebbed windows of a wine-cellar. He was at Eton and at one of the Universities, and has brought away from his college career one quotation—*Nunc est bibendum;* one mathematical axiom—the whole is greater than a part; and one economic truth—supply is equal to demand. His lordship has as yet always found it so; if he does not invariably obtain the whole, he has never been known to take less, or not to desire more than he can get; and if his translation of "*nunc*" be peculiar and somewhat extensive, it may be urged in his defence that "now" is his normal state. He would be always harmless, if he were never drunk; and quite at a loss what to do with himself, were he ever to find himself sober. Nature gave him a title and a good digestion, both of which she has refused to many a better fellow.

What were they all doing? Well, everybody was talking, and nobody listening; everybody

contradicting everybody, without anybody knowing it. They were opening bottles, filling
glasses—sometimes breaking them—and trying
to injure each other at unlimited loo. I don't
think there was one man there, who, to whatever stage of sottishness he arrived, could ever
be blinded to the fact—if the fact arose—of the
pool being undividedly his. There would always
be that lode-star left. They would cling to
that as some drunken men will to the keyhole.
Gain was to them the sheet-anchor in an otherwise altogether weltering world. So long as
they went on playing, that rift of reason would
be left ; once they stopped, that little would go,
and they would rise from the card-table, and
forthwith be as drunk as folding-doors. I forgot:
there was an exception. Exception to them in
everything ; exception, in that beautiful face ;
exception in the great gift of genius ; ay, and
exception in being alone so thoroughly " gone,"
that he went on playing and losing till, now that
he had nothing more to lose, he could not even
be made to understand it. The exception was
Reginald.

" I never saw such a fellow as Vavasour," one
was saying ; "promised to come, didn't he,
Morley ? "

" Yes ; of course he did."

" And he never turns up, and keeps
Grafton away too." (The sound of a closing
door.) " Egad, that'll be him." He it was.

Surely, no one is thinking that Cyril Vavasour
at all affected to be superior to the jovialities—
noisy follies, if you like—usual with that part of
the population whose blood is still warm with
youth ? He was not at all ashamed to be, neither
am I at all ashamed to relate that he was at
this time, as I have explained, more severe in
his morals than most of his peers ; but *casti-
gator morum* neither at this time nor at any
other was he, or did he assume to be. And
if Time, that brings about such unexpected
changes, could ever invest him with that character, I should leave his history to be concluded by some more ardent sympathiser with
superior virtue, as I much prefer to narrate
men's mishaps than angels' impeccability. And
even with these extravagant roysterers he was

somewhat of a favourite. Would he not sit down? Would he not put into the pool? Why was he so late? Where was Grafton? To all which questions he returned such answers as were truthful. He saw that his new companions were rather too far advanced on the road to excess for him to join them now with much hope of comfort to himself; but I think he would have made the effort for a time, and trusted to the chapter of accidents for an opportunity to get away by-and-by, had not the pitiful state of Reginald held him back. "You will be kind to Reginald?" Sobered sufficiently by Cyril's appearance to wake to his bankruptcy, he was not sufficiently sober to know how to hide it; and in a tone of plaintive bravado began swinging a little trinket backwards and forwards, offering to put it into the pool.

"Nonsense, youngster!" Morley called out; "there's money for you!" flinging it across the table. "You'll lose it like the rest, but go ahead." Something seemed to have happened to have changed Cyril's intention. No; he

would not play—he would look on. Yes; he
would help himself. All right. They were to
go on, all of them. He would rather watch.
Gradually, he brought himself nearer Cyril. I
scarcely think he was watching the game very
closely, though his eyes were fixed on something or other upon the table. Reginald again
was empty-handed. Cyril said he must go.
Would not Reginald go with him ? After some
remonstrances from the party, away the two
went. They were standing in Piccadilly.

"You had better go home. Cab!—Have
you any money?" (No intelligible answer.)
"Never mind, I'll pay him. Stay; I will, if
you'll give me that little trinket—the one you
had in your hand just now. No, no, no—not
that. Yes—there—give it me."

He told the cabman where to drive to. But
scarcely was the cab out of sight than he hailed
another, and himself went rapidly in the same
direction. He pulled up at the corner of the
street where Reginald lodged, saw him arrive,
saw the door open to his knock, saw him
admitted, and then walked slowly away. At

that very hour, Mary would be kneeling and praying for her boy-brother. The fond artist-sire, perhaps, was praying with her. Which were the more thrown away ? Their prayers, or his endeavours ?

But that little golden heart ! Conjecture was idle ; he would *know* to-morrow. He went to his chambers, wrote simply, "Dear Reginald, come and see me to-morrow. Yours affectionately ;" left it on the table for the laundress to post the first thing next morning, and went to bed.

The afternoon of that next day, about three o'clock, Reginald called. Cyril was writing. On the table was the heart.

"Hallo ! Where did you get this ? It's mine."

Cyril looked up.

"Where did I get it ? Had you been last night as you are now, you would know I got it from you. You gave it me."

"Gave it you !—don't remember. You'll give it me back ?"

"No, indeed. I want to know where *you*

got it ; that is the only reason why I asked you to call on me."

" Why—I—I scarcely know where I got it. I—er—think"——

" Look you, Reginald ! You do know. Why can't you tell me without ridiculous prevarication ?"

" Well, some one gave it to me ; a friend of Morley's."

" A girl. I don't ask you anything more than what is her name, and where she lives. I have my reasons for asking—reasons which do not concern you—so tell me."

" Well, she did not exactly give it me, you know. I took it to put on my chain. I knew I might, and intended to show it her."

At another time, Cyril might have indulged in a moral storm at this somewhat peculiar method of obtaining possession ; but now he contented himself with an impatient—

" Never mind *how* you got it ; but whose is it ? "

" Her name is Miss——or," he stammered, " Mrs. Tallington."

" And she lives ? "

" In Sussex Street, No. 149."

" Very well, thank you ; that's all I wanted
you for."

" But—but, I should wish her to know that
I took it away as—as I did."

" You appear to be on such intimate terms
with her, that I have no doubt you will have
an opportunity of explaining a proceeding that
she will in all probability think requires an
explanation. But I am going there now.
Perhaps you would like to come with me ? "

No, he could not ; he had a class—in fact, he
was late—he must go. And he hurried off.
When had he ever shown an anxiety for class
before ?

Mrs. Tallington was at home ; she was going
into the Park for a drive. If Mr. Vavasour
would take a seat, she would be down directly.
The door opened hastily, and she entered.
To Cyril there could be no mistake. Six years
had elapsed. Before him stood one of the
handsomest and most stylishly-dressed women
in London ; but, for all that, before him stood

the Tiny Forde of the little third-floor back in Somerset Street. Did *she* leap back as readily through the intervening time ? I think that faltering step, that rush, that pause, that catching of the breath, ay, and that blush—blush that, surviving the shame of years, mounted at the presence of a remembered love—that these, these proved she felt she halted in the presence of the ambitious boy whose despondency she had cheered, whose painful hours she had nursed, and whose disappearance she had so bitterly, so tearfully deplored. Six years ! To you—to me—a paltry interval. But the six years that intervene between sixteen and twenty-three! Surely these are " eternity to thought." Decades of suffering, ages of passion, centuries of sin would leave that marvellous sex faith in their earliest concession to the charms of the other ; ay, and imagination to drag it back and deck it anew from the very dust of the dissipated years. But we—we with our practical devotion to self—we with our wavering worship between the attainable and the ideal—can give to the retrospect of time, if intolerants, a sneer ; if philosophers, at most a smile. Well may she pause in that rush instinctively begun ; well may she check that thrill impossible wholly to repress ; for that motionless Cyril is *not* the Cyril of the past.

"I speak," he said, "to—to "———

The coldness of his manner recalled her.

"You speak, Mr. Vavasour, to Mrs. Tallington."

She took no seat ; she offered none. She let him stand hat in hand. She was dressed for her drive ; her brougham was at the door. His manner proclaimed that not remembrance of the kindness of other days, not desire to renew it in these, had brought him to her hearth. Let him speak his will.

"I have brought you back your property. Do you recognise it ?" He held out the little golden heart. With tremor she took it ; with tremor she answered him.

"Of course I recognise it. With no little concern I thought it lost. May I ask how you came to have it a—a second time ? It is very singular."

"No, not very singular; indeed, it is simple enough. I got it from Reginald Dormer. I came not to see if Mrs. Tallington was—pardon me—Tiny Forde; curiosity has nothing to do with my visit. Neither have I come in order to restore in person a trinket of such paltry value. I could have sent it you. I came to see if Mrs. Tallington, whoever she might be, would grant me a favour. Now that I have discovered who she really is, I scarcely think I shall be refused."

"Will you name it?"

"That you forbid Reginald Dormer your house. That he is here oftener even than I suspected, I see by traces everywhere visible in this room. I know his sketches; those "—he pointed to the walls—"and these "—he pointed to the table—"are surely his? You will ask me doubtless as to my right to interfere. Remember, I only ask a favour; but I will tell you why I ask it. He has a father, he has a sister; they are poor, and they love him. The knowledge that he comes here at all would break the heart of the one; the result of his coming here—excuse my frankness—will probably break the purse of the other."

She started as if stung. She stamped her foot hastily, and as hastily replied—

"Hah! Ever so! Wronged always—even by those who, if memory belonged to men, might suspect at least that I am not all selfishness. No, sir, *I* shall not break that father's purse any more than I broke yours before." He would have interrupted her in her terrible rebuke. "No, no, permit me my justification. You claimed frankness; allow it me in return. Do you want those sketches? You shall have them, at a gift, though I have paid (handsomely, I am told) for them all. It does not become me, when you are so outspoken, to injure myself by a modesty to which I have no right. From this house Reginald Dormer has never departed poorer than he entered it; nay, let me say it, he has gone away not unoften richer, without even leaving the, to me, valueless substitute of a sketch. You may question the worth of my kindness to the boy, as you perhaps question the worth of a by-gone kindness to yourself,

sincerely if injudiciously bestowed ; but at any
rate, if his acquaintance with me will press
heavily upon the sister's heart, you may find
compensation in the knowledge that it has at
least made lighter the pressure on the father's
purse."

Could he have answered her, scorn for scorn,
his sense of justice had been strange indeed.

"Tiny ! Tiny ! I did not come here to thank
you ; but that does not prevent me from being
grateful. You were once very, very good to
me. God bless you for it—though the prayer
here may sound an empty one. I can do no
more ; again I thank you." She covered her
face. "Nay, I will not indulge in superfluous
sentiment. I say again, I came here to ask a
favour, and I will not willingly go without its
being granted. Forgive my allusion to selfish
motives ; I did not require to be told what you
have told me now in order to be assured that
you are capable of what you esteem to be generosity. But generosity such as yours to that
self-loving boy will only complete his ruin. Forget the father's poverty ; but think of his love ;

and if that cannot convince you, you, who are a woman, think of his sister. To her I am under pledge to guard him as I best can. That pledge alone could have brought me here. I should not have come to acknowledge past kindness, though being here, I confess it, and would fain repay you."

She uncovered her face, and trembled towards him. "You *can* repay me. Look at me here. I am well cared for, surely. I lack nothing but happiness; I seek nothing but a friend. O Cyril, one quiet evening—one evening, such as many we have spent in that little room in Somerset Street, and I should have found both. Your last written words"—

"They spoke of home, and mother; they were little heeded."

"I have—I had—no mother, no home; but I had—bah!—beauty and despair. Come and comfort me; comfort me, Cyril! as, little knowing it, you comforted me so often before. You cannot be deceived in what I ask : I ask you to be only my friend! You think I love you. I have not said so. I can act many parts. I

shall not fail in a new one ; and you, surely you
can easily persuade yourself that an outcast such
as I am is incapable of love.   Yes, yes, believe
it ; but Cyril, give me your friendship ; believe
that I shall prize that ; believe that with that I
shall be fully satisfied.   Grant me that favour,
and the one you ask is granted too."

"Tiny, it cannot be.   You ask what I have
not the power to grant.   If you will show me
how I can help you to abandon your present
career, my help you shall have ; that once
honestly abandoned, you shall have my friendship.   Till then you shall have—for I can offer
—nothing.   I cannot seek your society here ; I
cannot accept it elsewhere.   Both are impossible.
My request is possible ; you will grant it ? "

She was silent a moment, looking meanwhile
steadily at him.   Then she said, resolutely—

" No, I will not."

"God help you, then !   I go."

" You go ; but you will return.   Each has
asked the other a favour ; both have refused.
Let us wait and see who will ask for the next."

＊   ＊   ＊   ＊   ＊

Marius amid the ruins of Carthage excites our profoundest sympathy; but what condolences shall we offer to the last man amid the ruins of the London season? Cyril, anxious to escape that mournful position, abandoned his chambers to his laundress, and turned his face in the direction of Alwoodley.

CHAPTER V.

IT was the first week in August, and the judges were still holding the Summer Assize at Onchester. Cyril had adhered to the scheme which he had propounded to Lady Harbledown. He had sufficiently satisfied himself and his parents that he really wanted to see something of the circuit practice of the profession to which he was to belong ; and for the rest, though silent on that topic, he was glad to be near the presence of Mary Dormer. He had taken lodgings close to the Minster, and not far from the Castle. In this last he spent most of the day ; not much absorbed in its legal proceedings, but still unremitting in his attendance, and certainly anxious that time would jog on apace. For his evenings were all spent either under the artist's roof, or in the green fields by which it was sur-

rounded. . From Mr. Dormer and from Reginald
too (who was at home) he received all the attention and hospitality which could be afforded in
their modest abode.   Generally both, nearly
always one of them, had accompanied Cyril and
his gentle companion in the eventide strolls which
were so charming a conclusion to the day's con-
finement in the ill-ventilated courts.   Twice it
had happened that they had been compelled to
take their summer ramble alone, and these, in
sooth, had been, to Cyril at least, the most
rememberable rambles of all.   It happened again
to-day.   Never had he been so happy as during
this visit ; never during the visit as on this,
almost his last evening.

How came it about, I wonder, that this boy,
whose custom it certainly was not to entertain or
weary his associates with his own feelings and
his own history, was marvellously communicative
when alone with the artist's daughter ?   It was
only by skill and expert questioning that even
Lady Harbledown had made him frank upon some
topics ; and even Stephen to himself sometimes
complained that the friend, whom he loved so

well in his manly fashion, had grown rather shy
of late in conceding his confidence. But with
this girl it was quite otherwise. Cyril told her
the story of his first acquaintance with London
with the fullest frankness, always omitting the
unhappy discovery which had driven him back
home perhaps a day or two before he had
otherwise returned. It certainly was not mere
egotism on his part that induced him to tell it,
since he ever shirked the subject when started :
nor was it blind conceit that led him to falsely
suppose that his listener was interested.

But his communications did not stop here.
Whether it was that in her presence dormant
restlessness was re-aroused, or that she, by some
undiscoverable influence, led him to avow sentiments which had never slept at all, but had
only assumed the mockery of slumber, I might
perhaps be pretending to know too much were
I to decide. Certain it is, that he made to her
the simplest avowal that the dreams which had
caused him to take the rash step which ended
in such signal discomfiture, haunted him still
with an undiminished—nay, with an accumu-

lated force. He had thirsted in his early boyhood for distinction; now in his youth the
thirst was strong upon him still. It had been
altogether unslaked by possession, and time
and waiting had only rendered it a more pressing passion.

We certainly have heard nothing of this of
late. Indeed, had I not occasion but a few pages
back to describe how dreams had departed, and
how money—money only—was his sole ambition? Am I to correct the passage? No: I
have been an honest and a faithful storier.
But, in our youth, the alternate presence and
absence of women work in us strange and
sudden and shifting revolutions. Like the
stars, the sunset, or the sea, the eyes looking
down on us of the Desired One suggest the
vast capacities which we have neglected or
forgotten, remind us of the powers we have
long allowed to lie in ignoble abeyance, and of
the immortality which by our grovelling indul-
gences we have ignored. What! shall we offer
to her a heart that throbs with aught less than
the beatings of a great, a lofty, a beneficent

ambition ? What! shall we ask to rest in her bosom a head that is not crowned with the laurels of a splendid success? Let us arise and walk in the footprints of the recorded; and then—not the millionaires of the market-place, not the Dives of the counting-house, nor the Fortunatus of a huckster's stall, but the surrounded of senates, the beloved of cities, or the darling of a nation saved, let us fling at her feet the fulness of our complemented fame.

I am going to write something of what passed between these two young people; and so I suppose I have fallen into a grandiose style which, it will surely be allowed, is more Cyril's than mine. And yet, by any less than pompous periods, I could not have described his present feelings. Clearly he was at the old game again; though now, perhaps, with the more practical aim induced by years and disappointment. Still he was for being great: and, in periphrastic language, of course, but which Mary thoroughly understood—and, it must be added, thoroughly admired—he told her so.

He had agreed to leave the Castle earlier than usual the following day, in order to accompany his friends to some ruins distant from Onchester about eight miles, and in great favour with Mr. Dormer. Finer August afternoon there never was ; finer type of the old monastic architecture had Cyril never seen. Yet his appreciation of the one, and his contentment with the other seemed forced to his companions, and were felt as such by himself. Something was evidently wrong ; and though nothing was said, they could not help wondering, and the pleasure of all was marred. Once Reginald asked if Cyril was unwell. No, he was not ; and there it ended. Poor Mary was puzzled and alarmed, and glad to be again at Onchester. She had not seen much of Cyril, it was true ; but the less she had seen, and was now likely to see of him, the less right surely had he to indulge those restless, uncomfortable, and discomforting—nay, half petulant—manifestations, which certainly had signalised his behaviour the whole afternoon. Would they continue during the entire evening ? What had she

done ?   Had she offended ; had she hurt him ?
The preceding evening had been the plea-
santest, the friendliest evening of all.   What
had intervened ?   They say that women are
specially gifted with penetration, and we need
not dispute the saying.   But, in this instance,
Mary Dormer scarce upheld the reputation of
her sex.   For who else does not see plainly
enough that Cyril Vavasour had arrived at that
stage of excitement, not peculiar to Hamlet,
in which a man thinks that if he holds his
tongue, his heart will very soon burst.   Women
very often refuse a man's request, very few
refuse flatly to obey a command.   So, when
skilfully inveigling Mary away from her father
and brother, Cyril *told* her to take his arm, and
led her still farther apart, it was not wonderful
that she did not demur.   I do not choose to
represent him exactly as he appeared in that
short walk.   There is a subject on which men
are more facile with their pen than with their
tongue ; and as he upon this subject employed
both, let us be content to see what use he made
of the more manageable weapon.   Yet, when I

think of it, letters are stupid, and love-letters are the worst of all. Let us be satisfied with the result. He has certainly written a sufficiently long letter, in all conscience. It is close on three hours after midnight. And yet, great Heavens! he is going to write it all out again—fair copy —before he goes to rest. Well, if boys would only do as much to win empires, as they do to win maidens, all our youth would wear the purple. Let him write. Mary had indeed confessed, in no passionate, but yet in quite intelligible, language, her preference for him ; but hearing from him the frank avowal that two—three— perhaps more—years would elapse before they could be to each other more than longing lovers, she had much pressed him to withdraw his confession, act towards her as though he had never spoken to her on the subject, and for the rest trust in God. She shrank from the troubles of the intervening years ; she dreaded the influence of delay, the accidents of time, the wounding of his heart, the breaking of her own. None of which arguments would Cyril either allow or understand. And what with his words, now grown more rapid than at first, and what with the pressure of his hand on hers, she had come to yield. They would write to each·other, and one at least would so be happy.

He had agreed to call some time the following day, the last he should have; and so, very early on in it, with the precious burthen (his letter) about him, he set forth. He thought he might have little opportunity of quiet private chat; and in any case, indeed, she must have the letter. Mary came down to the study, with her pale face paler than he had ever seen it. He gave her the letter; she put it down. She was very glad he had come, she wanted much to see him. She had not slept; she had lain awake and thought. She must repeat her scruples; she had yielded to his arguments last night, he must now yield to hers. No, they must *not* write to each other; they must not now be more than friends—not now, not now; what might hereafter happen let God see to. Surely he could understand her. He was not refused; he had not spoken his love at all—that was how he must consider himself placed. It was a question of prudence—of conscience. No, no, no; she could not yield. It must be even so.

He pleaded eagerly; he pleaded passionately. Life was at best a difficult struggle. Would she not make it easier for him by granting him the consciousness that he loved and was loved? Might he not have the encouragement that would arise from the knowledge he worked for *her?* The more he urged, the more she was firm; to him, it seemed the more cold. He talked rather wildly. Life had become sterile, was without object; he would go. No! friendship was no satisfaction; in fact, would be intolerable after he had aimed higher and missed. Oh, blind dolt! He left her; left her indeed much doubting (to judge from his last words) whether he would ever return.

However, about eight that evening he sought Mr. Dormer's. Mary looked pale and miserable; but from a glance Cyril saw that she had kept her secret and his own. She brightened at his advent. He sought the first opportunity of saying to her :—

"I had intended not to return; your wish has prevailed. I will accept your decision. If I ever have the right to ask for more than your friendship, I will ask for it; if gained, I shall have gained what I most covet; if not, I shall try manfully to bear the denial. Meanwhile, I trust in God, and am your friend. Are you satisfied, Mary?"

She answered simply—

"I have good reason to be," and it ended.

At half-past nine, Cyril rose to go; indeed to say good-bye, for that visit at least. In about half an hour more he would have to start homewards. Between Onchester and Alwood-ley was no railway; and even the coach, on which he had booked himself a seat, would leave him ten miles to post alone. So he should spend the night in the inn at Garstone, and drive in for church the following morning (Sunday). There he should meet his family, and so get himself and traps conveyed to Alwoodley. They were all very sorry he was going, they said; in another year he would be called to the bar, and they would then see him whenever the assizes brought him to Onchester. They were standing in the hall, saying the last adieus.

"You must not forget your coat," said Mary.

She held it as though she would help him to don it. It was an August night; but for all that he put it on, and even stood submissively looking down on her whilst with her delicate tiny fingers she fastened those large rough buttons across his chest. Oh, what would he not have given to have stooped and kissed that darling head, to have enfolded it in his arms and held it to his heart! He pressed her hand and departed.

CHAPTER VI.

A QUEER MEETING—A CRASH.

AFTER a cheerless ride, and with a not over-cheerful heart, Cyril arrived at the inn at Garstone. He thought a fire might mend matters ; he had ordered one, and was now sitting meditatively before it. His meditations were intruded on by the entrance of a man, who returned his look of examination with a stare far more inquisitive and prolonged, then threw a knapsack down upon the sofa, dragged a chair to the fire, stretched his long, stalwart legs along the hearth, and exclaimed :

"Such a stubborn beast! Fought it out with him as long as I could, and then gave in. He went kindly enough in the shafts all the way from Onchester till within a mile of this place, when not an inch further would he stir. I tried the *argumentum baculinum*, or whipcord argument—not mentioned in Aristotle, I believe, but sufficiently well known to the Schools—all to no avail. He answered me by several vicious circles; what could I do with so unfair an opponent? I threw up both the dispute and the reins, sent the gig back to Onchester, and came on here on foot. Have you ordered supper?"

Cyril said he had.

"Pity; you ought to have supped with me."

"There is no difficulty. We can have what they provide, together."

"No, no, no. You shall be my guest, or I yours; I don't care which, but one of the two."

"Then be mine, as I was the first arrival. See; we can set to work. I too came from Onchester, and am fasting."

His guest was a man of (in round numbers) forty: tall, strongly-built, handsome; dark, but with iron-grey plentifully mingled in his black hair. Gentleman he seemed in speech and ease of manner; but gentleman of a singularly

abnormal kind—gentleman in the teeth of
canons, and the circumscriptions of an arbitrary
civilisation.   Examined closely, his clothes were
intensely shabby ; but his splendid figure, and
lordly, indifferent way of carrying it, would have
prevented many observers from examining at
all.   Cyril could not help remembering that he
had noticed, walking along the road, with a knapsack, a man of striking resemblance to his new
companion, but certainly considerably more
than a mile distant from Onchester; and further,
that the coach had met no such gig as he
described to have sent back.   Still, with whatever humour of language he made the assertion,
could it be other than true ?

Though Cyril declared himself to be fasting,
he did not do very complimentary justice to the
viands of the landlord of the Greyhound ; but
his shortcomings were thoroughly made up for
by his voracious friend.   Supper over, they again
wheeled round to the fire.

"Capital idea of yours, this fire. *Tenui
meditaris avena?*—you indulge in a short
pipe ? Pardon my latitude of translation. I

dare say the eclogue was expounded differently to you at school; but commentators have not yet lost their rights. You *don't* smoke? I may, of course?" And he filled a pipe, drawn from his pocket and coloured by all the care of a connoisseur.

"So you too come from Onchester?"

"I do, to-day. I have been attending the assizes there."

"Professionally?"

"Well; yes—and no. I am not called to the bar yet; but I have been seeking some experience in the profession to which I shall belong."

"Hah! I looked into the courts once or twice. A very heavy calendar of prisoners, surely? Ill-informed philanthropists talk of the diminution of crime; the statistician knows that it does not, and the philosopher that it cannot decrease, under the systems and ideas predominant."

"I certainly heard it allowed on all hands that there had never been more prisoners. Most of them too were old offenders, and so penal servitude was the sentence of the majority."

"Yes; but not penal servitude for life. That would have reason in it, were the sentence carried out; for the struggling population would thus be diminished, and what remained would have the advantage of lessened competition. Yet the tendency of population to prevail over provender would soon bring about the same state of things, and a large drafting of men and women to penal servitude would again be required. So that from this view it would be more logical and more effective to circumscribe marriage or to drown babies." Cyril looked at the speaker, who puffed at his pipe, but was as serious as either of the judges under whom he had recently sat. "They who object to forbid the banns, or to baptise and decimate babies in the same bucket, are bound to look out for something better than penal servitude for restoring equilibrium."

"But," said Cyril, somewhat puzzled, yet feeling bound to make a remark, "you forget surely that we punish them because they have done wrong."

"Oh, no, we don't," he answered quickly, but without raising his eyes from the fire ; "we punish them because they have done something inconvenient ; in other words, for our own convenience. A perfectly justifiable ground—I don't deny it for an instant—but it is the fact. Were it otherwise, look you, we should punish vices as well as crimes, which we do not, as you must well know. Let us therefore be logical and reasonable with ourselves. We punish, I would rather say we treat, criminals according to our convenience ; it behoves us, therefore, much to see if we are really doing the best for our own convenience. At most, we only keep things as they are, at a great expense ; the same number of sessions, of assizes,—indeed we have had to increase these last ;—the same number of criminal judges, at the same salaries, from year to year without change or amendment."

"Then you think punishment useless ? "

"Perfectly ; and I will tell you what I think

equally so—preaching. Pensions would be more effectual than either or both. Pulpits and penal servitude have failed to keep poor men's hands out of rich men's pockets. Priests and gaolers have had their trial and have failed; let political economists have theirs. We have had a great deal of morality; suppose we try money. What say you to a new code and a new religion,—a religion in which '*facias rem*,' and 'not worth but money makes the man, the want of it the fellow,' will be the favourite texts; and a code in which people will be hanged, or at least transported for life, for marrying wives or having children whom they cannot support? So would our theories be consistent with our facts, and legislation be raised through the means of an honest induction to the dignity and usefulness of a science. We throw overboard readily enough the manners and customs of other periods, whilst we preserve their moral precepts, which fit us even worse. We strain our faculties in order to maintain in cities the decalogue of the Desert, and to keep inviolate in an age of money the maxims of an age when there was none."

"But surely—if you are serious—morality never changes : there are principles which are immutable truths, which are immortal."

"Ah, my good friend, beware of immortal truths! I have buried many in my time. It is not pleasant to be the sexton to one's own abortive opinions, especially when one feels no promise of a more perfect parturition. Abortive opinions are like other abortive births, they weaken and disfigure the frame, which, had they arrived at maturity, they would have strengthened and adorned. Morality never changes! We hear of fashionable vices—not of fashionable virtues : but the latter exist no less than the former. Looking through history as well as around me, I find a morality which has its sanction in the convenience of the majority. The talents that exalted Mercury into a god, now-a-days sink Smith into a felon : the wit that won the former a place in a mythological Walhalla, carries the latter into a matter-of-fact dock. Personal strength used to conquer

crowns : it now subjects you to an indictment
for assault and an action for damages. In the
heroic days, if you were weak you were kicked ;
now, you are coddled in an hospital, or propped
up with a subscription. Morality not change!
Of course it does : the mischief is, we will not
allow it to change enough. The facts have
changed—that is certain enough : them we cannot master. Preach from a million pulpits as
you will, one day in the seven, against the lust
of mammon-worship, there comes from the
crowded cities and from the fallow-fields, on the
other six, one huge contradicting voice, proclaiming aloud the new and only commandment
—Thou shalt not be poor !"

Cyril was silent. The words had come from
the speaker with consummate ease : he had
used no gesticulation, and he had kept his pipe
alight. Clearly, his language was the result
either of profound conviction, arising from long
meditation, or of a scorn so subtle, that it
assumed the aspect of an unflinching faith.
After a considerable pause, he said again :

"You are not convinced? You still think

that the principles of the human heart are ever the same. Let us take an instance which you, as a young man, will be sure to care for. Take Love—the love between the sexes."

"Surely that has not changed?" exclaimed Cyril, rousing himself at the mention of that tie which had for months so tempered the tone of his own mind, and just now monopolised, at least indirectly, the aim of his every thought and every action.

"Not changed! I can think of nothing that has changed so much. A history of the relationship of the sexes would be the most valuable of contributions to Philosophy: it would be nothing less than the history of the gradual, and as yet far from completed, enfranchisement of one-half—the larger half, by the way, as statistics show—of the human race from the tyranny of the other. I cannot pretend to present even an epitome. But at last we have hit upon the idea that woman may actually be a companion, the nurse of our ill humours and the supporter of our spleen. This is the highest stage to which she has yet arrived. She will yet advance. *You* may have to make love in the now accepted fashion ; but the next generation will no more think of winning their wives at morning-calls, pic-nics, balls, or twilight rambles, than you think of winning yours by publishing sonnets, threatening to poison yourself, or carrying her off at midnight into the marshes. The relationship between the sexes will have changed : more and more equality will the one have gained, more and more tyranny the other lost. Men will have to seek in women for friends and partners; not, as now, for toys, victims, or invalids. See—my pipe is out, and the fire soon will be. It is time to go to bed. Look you—my nonsense about the gig was all moonshine. I walked here, just as I shall walk away *from* here. I got you to ask me to supper, because I could not afford one myself. I was born a gentleman, as you must see, since you were evidently born one yourself. My name is Guy Blacklock. Before you go in the morning, pay my bill as well as your own. If we ever meet again, I will do as much for you, if you want it (which is not probable), and if (which is still more improbable) I have more money than I have now. Good-night! and thanks for your entertainment and your talent for listening."

He took his candle and departed. At another time an adventure so singular would have set Cyril pleasantly wondering. At another time, when the mere wonder at the new acquaintance had been satisfied, the novel opinions would have set him unpleasantly thinking.

He certainly did not go forthwith to bed; he mended the fire; he sat before it; but he had soon quite forgotten both the stranger and his sentiments. How can you expect a man who is in love to care about his fellow-creatures? What was penal servitude to Cyril? Surely the question whether millions shall be fed or flogged, trained or transported, is but of infinitesimal importance compared with the question whether the girl you worship is thinking of you or not at that identical moment? At any rate, the latter was the question which Cyril was at present entertaining. He entertained it for a long time, but had at last to go to bed without a solution.

The next morning he breakfasted alone, asked for his bill and that of Guy Blacklock, paid both, and started. He was in time for church, seemed to pray thereat very earnestly, and, it over, drove with his mother to Alwoodley. Was it his silence that made her silent?—she generally had many words. To-day she was as reticent as himself. When they reached Alwoodley, she took his hand, led him into the library, closed the door, and walked to the mantel-piece. He thought it very odd. She still kept his hand, and looked into his face.

" Can you bear bad news, Cyril ? "

" Yes, yes—well, well—what is it ? "

" We are ruined ! " she said, and burst into tears.

" Ruined ?—ruined ? How ruined ? "

" We have not a penny in the world."

" Pooh, mamma ! You always——"

The door opened, and Philip entered.

" What is all this stuff I hear from——"

" Now, my good fellow ! do be calm. It is

all true. My father owes 25,000*l.*, which he has no means of paying."

"But you—you—how long has this been so? Did you not know it?"

"I discovered it last Thursday. You know I am not a partner, so had no means of knowing. I discovered it by opening a business letter in my father's absence, and forced him to tell me the whole truth. All that we have got to do is—to be quiet and bear it."

❊   ❊   ❊   ❊   ❊

Four months later, over the December slush, and in the December sleet, was Cyril Vavasour being slowly driven through those Alwoodley gates which he had once slung passionately behind him. Opposite him sat his mother, in her widow's weeds: opposite him sat Philip, with his dark, defiant face. In the rear came trailing along another equipage, occupied by the father, all alone. Mournfully fell the sleet,—mournfully fell the prayers,—mournfully fell the creaking of the lowered coffin on the ears of the sobbing sons. The widow of that money-murdered man heard none of these; but on her

heart fell the weight of that desolation which
not even the recollection of how she had tended
him, loved him and been loved by him to the
last, could either dissipate or diminish.

CHAPTER VII.

"SHE gave me the number of the box on Sunday," Vavasour was saying aloud to himself, as he read the first page of a note just received; " I knew well enough Thursday was the night. What ? ' Whether it was that I was very tired and out of sorts yesterday I don't know, but I had such an awful dream à *propos* of the person whom we had been talking about, and who has formed the subject of one or two conversations, and you were using the strongest language, which I wonder how I could have got into my head— in the dream of course—so that I was prevented seeing the end of it by awaking frightened. We will not discuss the subject again, I think, for it only makes me talk of a person with a sort of apparent want of respect, which he is far from deserving ; but I should like you very much, if

L

you had the time, to write me your opinion on
the subject in the form of a letter, so that once
and for all I could have your words always by
me, for if any could influence me it would be
them, spoken so kindly and truthfully as you
speak them—already I have wavered a little
bit—and then you know we need never mention
it again.

  "' Believe me, yours sincerely,

     "' BLANCHE LATIMER.

  "' I trust you will see nothing strange in this.
I half regret writing it; but I cannot help
having confidence in you.' "

  He threw it on the table.

  " Bah! what do I care? She has spoken to me
on the subject, and I must say something; and
having no reason for doing otherwise, I say
what I think. But I don't see why I should be
condemned to write about it; however, away
at once, if it is to be done. And Blanche is a
jolly girl, very kind, and devilish intelligent.
But what a note! Composition very indifferent,
not like her conversation; punctuation, of
course, quite out of the question."

He sat down, and wrote a long but hasty letter. It was a dull performance : it was on a dull topic—the question of duty—so I will not reproduce it. The advice simply amounted to this : that the sooner she found out her own mind, the better ; and as soon as she had found it out, the sooner she gave it to the poor patient man in India, about whom she wrote again, the better. He should probably look in at the Opera on Thursday, and was Miss Latimer's sincerely.

Had Mr. Latimer arrived—Box H, second tier ? Yes. Was it full ? No ; only three in it. All right : take him to it. The box-keeper led the way. Vavasour peeped in. It was all right ; only old Latimer and one of the brothers with *la belle* Blanche.

" Very glad to see you, Mr. Vavasour. Any news ? See : take this chair." The old boy was really always very civil.

" Yes, I have news, though bad news ; that is why I looked in on you." (Scarcely true, eh ?)

" Oh, but you'll stay ? No one else is coming ;

or if one of the boys does, he must find friends somewhere else. But what is the news ? "

" News that Miss Latimer will not be glad to hear. Lady Harbledown remains in Italy this summer, if not longer."

" Remains in Italy ! Are you sure ? "

" I have her own assurance. See, I have brought her letter : I will read you that part after the overture commences. But the fact is, that Sir Wilfrid is so displeased at the threatened opposition in the county, which they say is sure to be successful, that he has determined to loll in the sun and the picture-galleries of the south."

Vavasour expected this news would be a severe blow to Miss Latimer's spirits, for it was certain that she had counted upon getting, through Lady Harbledown's protection, introductions which without her would certainly not be obtained. To his surprise, she seemed to be but little, even if at all, disappointed ; nay, supposing her sincere in her countenance, and him capable of translating it, it was not without something like joy that she turned it from the information towards the stage. "Don Giovanni" was the opera.

"Why do women," said Miss Latimer, when the act was over,—"why do women come to theatres, to operas more especially, and this one still more particularly? Is it to see their sex degraded?"

"You speak as if you did not belong to the sex."

"It is my misfortune, not my fault; do not taunt me with the accident."

"Not I, surely. But you,—you regret the accident?"

"Certainly I do. Is it a fine thing to be one of the *mille e tre*?"

"Well, no. But are you contemplating the addition of another to that distinguished corps?"

"Hush, sir, with your wilful and malevolent misinterpretations. You know I speak of the sex to which the '*mille e tre*' belong; it is only in the light of '*mille e tre*' that we are represented here. That is why I ask why women come to see themselves thus pourtrayed?"

"Oh, but wait. Let us come again on Saturday, and you shall find heroines who are saints and martyrs."

" Yes, when we are not represented as wicked, we are represented as absurd."

" And you find the choice difficult."

" I did not say so ; but why may we not be fascinating without being—what shall I say ?— Circes : or models of virtue without being burned or idiotic ? They say that the theatre is a teacher. I think that in theatres we learn little. For life is not a series of grand stage-effect heroisms, but of small back-slum sacrifices."

" True, as an assertion, but not as an argument. If women did not come to theatres, they would positively know nothing of realities ; as it is, they don't know much."

" But you don't mean to say that the representation of life on the stage is truer than the life we see off it."

" *Who* see ? Not truer than the life *I* see ; but considerably truer than the life *you* see. In a mock-decent and hypocritically decorous age like ours, theatres are required to remind men and positively to inform women of human nature.

Omitting broad farce, our plays approximate pretty closely to representations of either life as it is, or life as it should be."

"And the life off the stage ? "

"Represents at once both life as it isn't, and as it shouldn't be."

"You are talking paradoxes. Why will you not be earnest ? Am I beneath your seriousness ? "

"I shall begin to think so if you don't understand me better. I was speaking *au grand sérieux* : you had positively entrapped me into an argument. But I will be as illogical as you like. Hush !—the trio ! "

The devils had disposed of the Don. Frank, the brother, had disappeared ; was in the omnibus probably ; and old Latimer was bent forward, quite intent on the commencing ballet.

"You don't care for that ? " asked Miss Latimer.

"Oh yes I do ; or should, if you were not here. *I* am not angry with my sex, or with yours."

"You are intolerable to-night—tsha! I got your letter."

"The post has arrived at marvellous perfection."

"Don't, Mr. Vavasour!" said so imploringly. He was standing over her chair. She turned and raised her head, as though she would have him lower his. He lowered it.

"Papa says I am behaving very badly to him," she whispered.

"To whom?—to your papa himself?"

"No, no; you know whom I mean." And she touched her India shawl (now turned into an opera-cloak) significantly. "Such a dream as you made me have."

"I! I can do more for you then than for myself. I never dream. Will you make me dream?" He touched — it wanted but the muscular action of his lips to kiss—her hair. And she? Must she not have felt it stirred by his breath, warmed by his words? It must have been the atmosphere of her tresses that made him add : "make me dream of you?"

She looked quickly at him, and saw upon the lips that had spoken a smile that puzzled—it should have warned her.

"I have no power to bring about either dreams or realities," she answered ; "you have power over both."

"I am not partial to either, unless they can be united. Give me the enjoyment of the one, with the evanescence and after oblivion of the other ; or my attributed power is valueless."

"As I have told you before," she said, with rapid consecutiveness in time, if not in meaning, " you will marry a pretty fool."

" Then it is certain I shall not marry "—he shrugged his shoulders—" you."

" We both know it. It was not necessary to draw the conclusion in words."

"I like *vivâ voce* logic."

" You like everything that is harsh."

" Then you do not come in the catalogue, 'il catalogo,—'" and he hummed the air from the opera they had just heard,—' "il catalogo delle belle che amo,' et cetera, as Lablache has been singing to us."

"No, I am not harsh; but there is no good in being gentle with you. What pleasure do you find in saying hard things?"

"My dear Miss Latimer! I only laugh: you must allow me that much freedom for a time. I will try and mend. Let me help you with the major's cloak—'tis just over."

"Thank you. Can we not take you part of your way? Oh, but you are going to the Temple."

"No. I am going to the House. There will be a long debate to-night, and I may have another half-hour's reporting to do."

"Why do you bother yourself with reporting?"

There was not a soul of his acquaintance in London who suspected that it was now his chief, if not sole, means of livelihood. Some fellows have a rich look, and a rich way with them: Vavasour was of these.

"To make money, of course."

"You don't want it: and it must be often tedious work."

"'Want' is a relative term: so is 'tedious.'

I like money, or what it brings ; and I am not so easily bored by toil as by talk. If I could only report without listening, I should not mind the work in the least. And then if I am to marry my pretty fool, I must make money quickly—quickly : must I not ? "

" Then go and make it. How is Reginald Dormer ? I never see him with you now. Bring him to call some day, will you ? "

" No ; he can please himself ; but I will not help him to be idle."

" Is our acquaintance necessarily productive of idleness ? "

" It would be to him. However, 'tis not my affair. I will see you to your carriage."

The House was still sitting when Vavasour entered the reporters' gallery, but broke up unexpectedly five minutes after his arrival. As he recrossed the lobby, a man seemed to hasten after him, but as he had had the start, and was walking rapidly, did not fairly overtake him till he was fully half way down Westminster Hall, and even then did not gain his side, though fully able to do so, but seemed to wait till they both emerged under the lamp of Palace Yard. For a moment it appeared that in again suddenly quickening his steps the man was about to pass on, when a rapid side look satisfied him and brought them abreast.

"I thought it was you, but could not be certain without a third look. I saw you first in the reporters' gallery ; I was in the strangers'. Then I waited for you in the lobby ; but there was such a crowd, and you were walking at such a pace. You remember me, surely ? "

"O dear, yes ; Guy Blacklock. I have not forgotten our supper : I am going to my chambers in the Temple ; come with me and I will give you another."

Vavasour's manner might not be very cordial : for his reception of people had altered much of late, having lost its old affectionate way of welcome ; but in reality no man had he ever met whom he had so often wished to meet again as this Blacklock. At the time of their delivery, he had listened with little interest—indeed with perhaps a little impatience—to his companion's sentiments : but the force with which facts, arising immediately after that strange conversation, had brought them home to him in his own case, had caused him often since to reflect on their signification, and no less on the odd personage who had so positively pronounced them. We are sure always to think much of the man who propounds a theory which explains the facts of our particular experience, just as each one of us prefers and praises that poet who most faithfully and frequently gives utterance to our individual sentiments. The capacity of making rapid inductions is the distinguishing feature of those who influence their kind, most minds merely demanding the shortest cut to some positive conclusion. All inductions, with our present limited knowledge, must be more or less wrong. But to gain mastery over men, and more particularly over women, it is not necessary to be right, only to be positive. It is fatal to a man's success to see both sides.

Though Vavasour expressed no satisfaction at meeting his friend of the Greyhound, he felt it ; and Guy Blacklock was not the man to

refuse a supper on account of the coldness of
the invitation.

"You paid my bill that morning; gentlemanly thing of you. You are in clover here,
wallowing in the fat of the land. I suppose
you are just as convinced as ever, from your
having plenty of it, that money is not of the
slightest importance? It is impossible for a
man who is *solutus omni fenore*, without a debt
in the world which he cannot pay, to be really
interested in the natural history of duns."
(Vavasour thought of his bills in Bond Street,
and laughed.) "It is a pity," continued the
other, "that you are not, or at least have not
been poor. Poverty is the only philosopher's-
stone; by it a man discovers what little by one
man can be known. I read of complaints that
the rich and the high-born add nothing to our
social knowledge. The complaint is ridiculous;
they cannot tell us what they have no means
of finding out. Suppose us all rich; we should
have a very well-behaved, but a very ignorant
and very uninteresting world; three-fourths
of our passions would be annihilated. What

makes modern city existence, to those who really know it, so intensely pathetic? Simply its wants, and its consequent struggles to satisfy them. What duller than the record of a pastoral tribe, each man with his so many sheep and so many sons? We tell young children of these things first, just as we feed them first with pap; stronger food either for head or stomach would be too stimulating, so we keep both for a later period. Money, with its multiplied manifestations, should be the study of him who would tell the century its own secret, and so become the wonder and instructor of the next. In the investigation of its influence and action, will the modern wizard find his wand. Let no one attempt to sing now-a-days of 'Arms and the man.' You remember the first ode of Anacreon. Well, that will not do either; the time for singing of love is also past. If, in our modern tragedies we have battles, it must be the battle of the banks; and, to use the recognised language of Aristotle's poetics, the revolution or discovery on which depends the transition in our Epopee, must be a sudden depreciation of the currency. You are young; profit by the hint, and be the Poet of the new period. You do not smoke, I remember; therefore you do not smoke here ; but do you allow others ? "

" Yes ; " said Vavasour, " smoke away ; only I cannot give you either cigars or tobacco. Ha, you have it. Thanks for your last suggestion : but when we first met, you were all in praise of money, now you seem to belaud the want of it."

" No, no, you have not caught me ; I am not so illogical. It depends on what you want. If you want what is called a virtuous, what I prefer to call a well-behaved world, you must be (as I asserted, I believe, on the occasion you refer to) an advocate for a universally rich world. But if you want a tragic (or comic,— they are much the same, it depends *how* you look),—if you want a tragic, an interesting, a pathetic world, a world worthy the study of the poet (and by a poet I always include the idea of philosopher), you will then advocate the unequal distribution of wealth ; a state of things

in which everybody desires to have money, and
very few have it. A universally well-off world,
would be either a world beginning again, or a
world worn out. You would occasionally have
an interesting murder, or an exciting elopement,
but your docks would be empty of charged
felons, your gaols of convicts, your streets of
outcasts. The admirer of a well-behaved com-
munity would proclaim the arrival of the millen-
nium ; but the student of human nature would
sigh for the records of a police-court, and the
blue-books of a hell. As I said, it all depends
upon what you want ; whether you regard the
economy of the universe with the aspirations of
a saint, or the sympathies of a Shakespere."

Vavasour's attention to-night was of a very
different intensity to that with which he had
listened to his guest on a former occasion. As
then, he still said little ; but what little he did
say was said with the purpose of making the
other discourse. He grasped eagerly at the
chance of finding a helping head in the
solution of perplexities that largely occupied
his own.

" So you think that the equal distribution of money would tend to prevent what we regard as mere vices, as well as what we regard as crimes ? "

" Surely.   Can I doubt it ?   An unfortunate would be as rare as a pickpocket or a footpad, in a world such as we talk of.   Look you.   I know nothing of your concerns.   You seem sufficiently comfortable for a bachelor; but you are young, and could not, I daresay, marry if you wished it."   Vavasour nodded assent. " Well, I will suppose—no extravagant supposition, even if it be not a true one—that you have at some period desired, or do at present desire, to marry some girl altogether suitable, and who would marry you could you keep her." Vavasour started.   " Well, you cannot.   Again I say, I know nothing of your concerns ; but I will suppose—again no extravagant supposition, even if again it be not a true one—that you are no better than your neighbours.   Now——"

" Suppose you leave my personal sores alone, and continue your argument in the abstract."

"Be it so. My touching the sore only shows that I am more right even than I had any suspicion of. Pardon me. But let no man think that his individual experience is a solitary one. A man who has discovered his own secret had better go and tell it to his neighbours, for it is their undiscovered secret too. There are thousands like you. *We* are sitting here; but how many young fellows are there at this moment, within a mile of us, drinking and lolling in saloons and supper-rooms, who, if they had had so many hundreds a-year more (or other people who give the tone to their society so many hundreds a-year less), would have been sitting with slippered feet on the domestic hearth, teaching their children the Lord's Prayer, or reading to their wives the Pilgrim's Progress?"

"To be frank," said Vavasour, "I have never heard you so weak before, and altogether so unconvincing. My experience—it is small, but it is positive as far as it goes—rises against you. I could name scores of men who are in a position to marry, scores of others who are married, whom you will find chief actors in the scenes you stigmatise."

" Quietly, quietly, my good friend! I have not convinced you, because I have not completed my argument. But I am glad you see, and have put, what objection remains, in so clear and tangible a form. So long as there are such scenes, there will be firstly many spectators, and afterwards actors, who did not participate in projecting the play. Many men will leave the lawful for the unlawful. But are we not going to do away with it? I think so, under our scheme. So many thousand sempstresses, laundresses, farm-servants, waiting to be—led astray, say you? Not at all; I answer,—fed! How many peers' daughters are befooled in a year? They are mere women like the others, with the difference—of a dinner: that's all. And in the world we talk of, there would be dinner for all; husbands for all. They who, in a world composed chiefly of poor people, are abnormally rich and consequently mostly without occupation, will of a certainty run the gauntlet of all experiences that are pleasant. Those experiences removed, they would necessarily confine themselves to the experiences that remained. It is the difference of fortune that favouring the lust of some, and forcing the hunger, or at least the covetousness, of others, gives us wandering women, prurient boys, unfaithful husbands, and unhappy wives. The necessities of the weak assist and are in turn assisted by the desires of the powerful. Were we all equally strong, we should all forbear from striking."

"But your equality, conclusively carried out, would end in a complete ——"

"Democracy; not a doubt of it."

"Do you think such possible?"

"Thank you. I will not discuss that question. This at least have I shown : that equality, or as you justly call it, democracy, will do away with nearly all (I *could* show, all) crime and vice; and that the only machinery which will bring about this equality, this democracy, is money. Let then those who are enamoured of a well-behaved—if they prefer the phrase, a virtuous—world, abandon bell, book, and candle, and stand honestly out full-blown democratic political economists. *I* have a weakness for the world as it is, and am off to have another look on it.   Good-night!"

"But you will come to see me ?   Are you living in London ?"

"Living in London!   Great heavens!   I should think not, indeed.   But I know now where *you* live, and likely enough you will see me again.   Thanks for your repeated hospitality."

"Stay ; do you want any money?   I am not rich, of a certainty ; but if——"

"No, no : if I accepted a sovereign from you now, I might be prevented in honour from out-witting you out of two on a future occasion, and that might be inconvenient.   No ; good-night!" And with his long, powerful arm he swung the outer door to, and departed.

"Who can the fellow be ?   The most polished Bohemian that ever stepped.   A gentleman, a scholar, a beggar, and to all seeming an out-cast ; an intense, if not a deep thinker ; a very Jaques, without his melancholy, but with superabundant scorn. Who *can* he be? I should like to know his history."

He went out on to the terrace in front of the Temple library, though it was after two, and walked up and down may-be half an hour, thinking doubtless all the while of the conversation which he had just held.

" Well ; bed now."

And he turned in towards his chambers.

" Never looked at the paper, to-day : I wonder if my laundress took it back. No, here it is ; nothing in it, I suppose. Great Conservative Meeting in Essex ; Maine Law ; Middlesex Sessions ; Lord John on the Ballot. Bah!—to-bed, to-bed. Great heavens! What? Regret to have to announce that Mr. Dormer, R.A., was found—good God!—dead in his bed yesterday morning. His unexpected decease is attributed to affection of the heart."

His hand and the paper containing the intolerable intelligence fell together to his side ; his mouth contracted ; and his eyes stared rigidly outwards on the moon that shone in through his open window : shone as it had shone

on the August night ten months ago when he
had bid Mary Dormer let it some night shine on
their love and their marriage-couch. What had
occurred since then? What had happened
him? I do not say, what had happened in his
heart, for we can take no true soundings there.
Its depths lie too far away for the poor
short plummet-line of our lame observations.
Perhaps from the colour of the surface we can
make some sort of guess at the deposits of its
clandestine distance; but that is all our most
patient skill can achieve. We can do no more.
Therefore, leaving altogether what may have
happened in his heart, I only ask what had
happened in his exterior life. We have seen,
for the most part: and what I have not mentioned till now, must at least have been readily
concluded. Who will not be prepared to hear
—perhaps some will accuse me of unnecessary
garrulousness if I say—that he had been doing
his best by silence to weaken the link which
existed between him and the Dormers, and
which he had once striven (how soon it afterwards appeared, fortunately in vain!) still more

to strengthen ? It had been his custom, during the year which elapsed between his first and second visit to Onchester, occasionally to send Mary Dormer periodicals and journals in which were written articles or were executed engravings that he could manage to persuade himself were likely to interest her. After but a single visit, this might seem a stretch of familiarity, though I am enabled to say positively that by that loyal little family it was not deemed such. But surely if, after one kindly period of intercourse, this delicate attention might without scruple be shown, there was every reason to expect that after a second visit, which, though not without interruption to its serenity, was also not without its compensatory assurances, and in which Vavasour at its very close asserted himself (while ambitioning in the distance to be something more) to remain meanwhile at least her friend—I say there would be every reasonable expectation on her side that the attention would be continued. But the post brought now no periodicals, no journals, no skilfully explanatory or apologetic letters for sending these, as heretofore. Not a line had been written, not a paper sent. Nay, more: Reginald had experienced from Vavasour an indifference about his presence never hitherto displayed, even when he had come to be lectured for past scrapes, or replenished in pocket for the getting into fresh ones ; and as he disliked the lectures, and found more money elsewhere, he only assisted Vavasour's cold distance by his own.

This is what had happened : what was to happen now ? He went to the window; he leaned out; he held his face against the air that already began to stir with restless suspicions of the dawn. It did not cool him. Again he went unto the Terrace, slowly pacing whilst the great city slept. Another hour had gone ; again he returned to his chambers. He sat down and wrote to Reginald, who would doubtless have rushed away to Onchester. He was generally impatient with his pen, and wrote rapidly ; to-night he was singularly slow in his sentences. The letter consisted but of commonplace condolences, and yet he was long in

shaping them. Oh! had he but been writing
the originalities which he so sternly repressed,
his hand had not halted so. Well, he had
nearly done. He should be happy to be of
what service he could. Reginald was to ask
his sister to share the sentiments expressed by
the writer; and Vavasour was always, but in
their sorrows most, hers as well as his sincere
and sympathising friend. He addressed and
sealed the letter; and with a face hard as the
faces of the monumental Templars, whose stone
effigies were in the church below, he lay down
and slept.

Had there not happened enough to make
the soft boy stern? Fortunately, his father in
dying left but one creditor, the bank that had
traded on his misfortunes, and had nothing to
gain by making them public. That he had
died poor everybody knew; but they knew no
more. Philip had gone to South America, as
partner in a firm but too glad to secure his
services, and had taken his mother with him.
Cyril was left to fight his way as best he could,
to bury his love, stamp on his ambition, keep

his head above water, and put a well-to-do
face upon it; all which he seems to be doing
pretty bravely. Was he better for it? Who
dares decide? At any rate he was harder.
The back was getting shaped to the burden.

CHAPTER VIII.

THERE is nothing that puts a man so thoroughly into good humour with himself, and
makes him so favourably disposed towards the
world generally, as the first stroll through the
west-end London streets after a long sojourn
in the country. Fresh eggs are very charming,
and Thomson's Seasons in the fields are sooth-
ing to the excited nerves after Terpsichore's
Seasons at the Opera ; but for all that one is no
more free from the charm of change than the
year itself, and one turns with a relieved ear,
eye, and heart from sermons in stones to sermons
in shop-windows.

Vavasour was taking *his* first look about him
after his return, and so was in that pleasant
frame of mind hinted at. Great admiration
for his own infirmities, and perfect toleration

at least for other people's, spoke out from his
tread, from the folds of his loose overcoat,
from the benevolent simper of his cosmo-
politan countenance. He dispensed largesse
among the crossing-sweepers with an uncalcu-
lating hand, though the ways were as clean as
his own spotless boots; dowered the organ-
grinders and the monkeys with silver three-
pennies, and positively felt tempted to bowl
about in a Hansom from mere *gaieté de cœur*.
This last temptation, however, he resisted ; and
had now gained the top of the vulgarest street
in Europe. Who asks if its name be Regent ?

"Well, you need not cut all your friends,
because you have been in the country six
weeks."

"Ho, Morley ! how are you ? Didn't see you.
But how is it *you* are not in the country ? "

"I am ; but I run up to get a little fresh air
in London every now and then ; and I come to
Regent Street to button-hole my friends and
walk off with them to Surrey. Come down to
us : I'll give you capital shooting, and lots of
good lush. Your friend Grafton is coming in

a fortnight; he is quartered at Canterbury again, and will have his leave."

"Yes, I know that. Well, you tempt me. I'll think of it. Let us walk down; it's cold, standing."

"Come along. By the way, have you seen anything of Reginald? No? His sister is coming to us to-morrow, I think, or the day after."

"I am very glad to hear it. I thought your people did not know her. It will be a change for her. I suppose Dormer died poor? With whom are they going to live, do you know?"

"Of course he died awfully poor. He had only one picture; a rattling good one, they say (I know nothing about it), but it was unfinished, and hasn't fetched much. And Miss Dormer is coming to us as governess to the young 'uns. Ha! ha! my good fellow! the cab was half-a-dozen yards from us,—no fear. What a start you gave! A fellow from the country ought to have his nerves in better order; but one soon grows unaccustomed to cab-wheels. Now, when will you come down?"

"Why—er—you see, I have been idling a good deal of late. I fear I must refuse your invite ; much obliged all the same. I must leave you here."

"Nonsense."

"Yes, I must, positively. I have to be at the Temple by a quarter to six. Good-bye, old fellow ! "

"You'll write to say when you'll come. I go back to-morrow. *Do* try."

"Yes, yes, I'll write, if I can come ; but—but —good-bye ! "

*   *   *   *   *

A nasty November fog had all day clung to the outskirts of Onchester, and, now that the night was closing in, availed itself of the favouring darkness to invade the suburban streets, and at length held in its pitiless possession the minstered city.

On the doorstep of what had been the artist's home, Vavasour stood and rang. The bell answered loudly to his hand ; it seemed as if it would never cease ringing. He could hear it pealing through rooms that must be empty.

When—when would it cease? When—when—
when would some one answer it? Was he too
late? The blinds were taken down; no fire
gleamed through the panes; the garden so
small, but always, when he had known it, so
strictly cared for, lay like an excommunicated
plot, the Golgotha of idiotic ghosts. At last,
feet on the passage pavement — a light — a
hand on the door.

"Miss Dormer : is she within?"

It was the dear old servant's face.

"Why—yes, sir; but she is going to start
directly."

"Say I am here—quick—quick!"

"Yes, sir; this way. There is a fire in the
little room that used to be master's studio. I
will go and tell her."

A fire; a deal table; nothing more. The
servant had even taken with her the candle.
He heard the rustle of a dress down the stairs,
followed by a short pause. Then the door opened
and closed, and in deep mourning, attired for her
journey—only the black veil thrown back—the
face still paler, the dark eye-lashes still more

tremulously closing and opening on the blue orbs than ever—Mary Dormer stood before him.

"You have only just caught me, Mr. Vavasour; I am very sorry to be going immediately; but there is no help for it. What brings you to Onchester? the assizes are not on, are they?"

"No, no, the assizes are not on; but—but—nay, can you not guess what brings me here? I come to prevent your journey."

"To prevent my journey! how can that be?" She looked at her watch. "I must start in ten minutes; but, if you will, you can see me, with Martha, to the coach."

"Mary! Mary! I am not the impassioned boy of sixteen months ago. I do not come to say to you warm fond words. God knows I said them all then! But I come at least to tell you what I have told you before: that I would offer you the home—of a wife. I have no wild way of asking now; frankly accept my offer as it is frankly made; and then—not before, for my tongue is tied—I will explain what may perhaps seem strange."

"Really, Mr. Vavasour, there is nothing to

explain. Who has accused you? Nothing to explain, except it be indeed this singular visit."

"I heard only yesterday of your plan—of your —your going to Mr. Morley's."

"Does that explain the visit? You come to save your honour. Really it is without taint, at least in my eyes. And if it be tainted in your own, or those of others (though I know not whose), will my becoming your wife purify it? Even if it will, is it not a little unreasonable to expect me to marry a man in order to save the sensitiveness of his self-respect? I have chosen an honest means of livelihood; be generous enough, Mr. Vavasour, to leave it me."

"But—but—Mary! Miss Dormer!—my love! —my—my——"

"I am surprised that you do not understand that there are some things which cannot be argued. Conviction is produced without logic. Indeed, I must be starting. You once promised to be my friend; I sincerely hope that you will still remain so."

The words were uttered loyally by her who spoke them, and in her breast was no suspicion of scorn or satire; but the recollection of his conduct during the months of her desolate condition, now so thoroughly brought home to him in this crowning spectacle of distress, sent them accurately to his heart, barbed with a sarcasm that was intolerable.

"Then—then—Heaven help us! You know not what you do," he said. He hurried away; and as he slung the gate to, and plunged into the mist, he heaved out,

"Well, God see to it; for she has marred the music of my life."

*   *   *   *

"Very well, very well; no, we won't be long. If we are, it will be the ungallant cornet's fault, and you may blame Grafton, not me.—Come, old fellow, now that the girls have gone, wheel round to the fire. That's your glass, isn't it? Fill up. What a jolly day we've had of it!— the best bag yet. Confound Vavasour for not coming down."

"Oh, I should think he'll come. I wrote to him last night, and used my influence—and I suppose nobody has more over him in such matters than I have—to accept your invitation. Dear old Cyril! there's no one like him."

"Yes, he's a capital fellow, though you speak of course as his great friend; but I like him too, very much, though he's too literary, and that sort of thing, for me. But I hope he'll come. He used to be so awfully pious about a year ago; but I think he has mended of that."

"Um, well, I think he has; but it's a very pardonable weakness, though not one that you and I, Morley, are likely to suffer from."

"Scarcely, my boy. Oh, by the way, I've written to Reginald to come down; *he's* sure to come."

"All the better. What a charming girl that sister of his is! You are certainly all of you very kind to her, and she's lucky to have found such friends; but still—dash it!—one doesn't like to see such a girl as that have to turn governess, you know, anywhere."

"Well, no; but what could she do? She certainly is a stunning girl, though not handsome, and very quiet, too; but there's a some-

thing about her—you know what I mean—a—
a—well, let us drink to her."

"I drink. She is not handsome, as you say ;
but she reminds me of what I once heard Cyril
say of some one else : that sorrow had made
her beautiful."

"That's a sentiment ; too much for me.
But Reginald once told me that Vavasour was
very fond of his sister, which is more to the
purpose."

"I don't think that. I dare say he liked her,
as most fellows would ; but he certainly never
said anything to me beyond that she was a very
nice girl."

"Oh, I don't mean that he was in love with
her, though I think Reginald fancied so. At
any rate, if he ever was, he certainly isn't now ;
nothing seems to satisfy him but Blanche
Latimer ; he's always with her. She's very
different : jolly enough ; but then she's awfully
clever, and sometimes beastly sarcastic. Since
your cousin, Lady Harbledown, has been
abroad, he has quite transferred himself to
her."

"He's only like the rest of us, fond of pretty women ; with this difference, that he can amuse them better than most of us can. And if a fellow can only get on well with them, it keeps him to a great extent out of other society less profitable and more expensive ; eh, Morley ? "

" Hit it, sir, exactly ; though some fellows succeed as ill in one as in the other. It was I brought Reginald across Lettice, and, hang it ! she has spoiled him ever since."

" Never introduce your friends anywhere. By the way, how about the Lampreys' ball ? you're all going, aren't you ? "

" I should think so. It's such a way for the girls to rush up to town, and come back again. I, of course, shall sleep in town, and I can give you a bed. No, by the way, I can't. I've promised to give one to Reginald, whom we shall take with us, if he pays his visit. Miss Dormer won't go ; as it is only six months since her father died. Reginald will, however. I'm sorry I can't give you a bed."

" Oh ! I couldn't have accepted it—thanks !

Cyril has promised me a shake-down; in fact, I shall dress at his chambers, and we shall go together. Well—let us go to the drawing-room."

"Miss Dormer has heard from her brother Frank," said Mrs. Morley, as her son and Grafton entered the room.

"Oh! indeed. What does he say, Miss Dormer?" And he walked over to where she sat.

"He thanked you for your kind invitation, and will be very glad to come."

"That's all right."

It was a large long room, with fire-places at each end: it was profusely furnished, taste being more or less sacrificed to consummate comfort. It was, in fact, a very lap of luxury.

"Yes," Mrs. Morley was saying to Grafton, "it is very hard for her, poor girl, but we do all we can to prevent her from feeling the painfulness of her position. We treat her exactly as one of ourselves, and, indeed, consider ourselves fortunate to have found so excellent a companion for our elder children, and so good a teacher for the younger ones. She is most amiable, and one of the best and most truly pious girls I ever saw."

" How long has she been with you ? "

" Let me see—Monday—Tuesday—yes, just a month to-day. Well—will you excuse me ? I must go to Mr. Morley. Poor man ! the doctors say there is no hope of his ever being anything more than the helpless creature he is at present—hopelessly paralytic. I think you had better not come up with me to-night to see him ; he seems much fatigued. I shall not be away very long. Mary, my dear ! "— to Miss Dormer—" order tea when you want it ; but I shall soon be down again."

Grafton addressed himself to the daughters : fair-haired, fair-visaged girls, with the Saxon complexion joined to the Norman physiognomy ; yet in them was nothing of that lofty look sometimes seen in countenances of the combined races. They were pretty, as such prettiness goes—no more. Frank Morley still sat at the other end of the room with Miss

Dormer, holding in his hand her brother's letter, which she had given him to read.

"I'm so glad he's coming. Do you know, I asked Vavasour to come too, but I fear he won't. He said he had wasted a good deal of time during the Long Vacation, and must work again. He's always working."

"Yes; I fancy that he is studious; he is very clever : is he not thought so ? "

"Yes; by everybody, I think; but he's rather—rather—what shall I say ?—visionary, and that sort of thing : at least, people say so. Did you know his father ? "

"No, I did not; but I have often heard him highly spoken of."

"So have I; but I fear he died rather in difficulties."

"Really ! "

"Yes; I fancy so : I have heard as much hinted at by our people in the City—but I know nothing. I should think Vavasour cannot have very much; but, as you say, he's a clever fellow, and, I suppose, sure to get on."

"I am very sorry to hear what you say : are you quite sure of it ?"

"About his father dying poor? Quite sure to that extent ; and not so certain that he was not a little embarrassed in business. You know the business was given up, and his elder brother is out in South America."

"Yes, I heard of Mr. Vavasour's brother going ; but I knew none of the family but Mr. Vavasour himself, and nothing of their—their concerns."

"Nor do I : only what I have heard dropped at the Bank, where you know I rarely go."

"Don't you think," she said, "that you ought to go more ? Don't you sometimes feel the want of occupation ?"

"Yes, I do ; but I shall, probably, be a sleeping partner, like my father before me. And then one has nothing to work for." He played with the letter. "If—if any one—if any girl—if you, Miss Dormer—were only to be sufficiently interested in me—to care for me—to make me go, I might improve. See —can you not care for me to that extent ?"

She looked up at him : he certainly had a very confused and yet earnest appearance. "You speak either in joke or seriously, Mr. Morley. If in joke, I do not——"

"Indeed, Miss Dormer, I never was so serious in my——"

"In that case I must ask—if necessary, insist—that you will not speak of it again. Hush ! enough has been said. I am very happy here : you are all most kind to me. Do not drive me away. I esteem you, Mr. Morley, as I esteem all your family : I shall never do more."

* * * * *

"Come, Stephen, old boy! don't be all night. There! you'll do. I shall charge you for keeping my cab standing. Wait : have I got my keys? all right : shut the outer door."

And the two friends rattled down-stairs to their Hansom.

"Sir Bedford Lamprey's—Chesham Place : and bowl away as quick as you like, cabby ! "

"You've no idea, Cyril ! how sorry the

Morleys were you didn't come down. We had capital sport ; and old Morley has stocked a tip-top cellar ; though, poor fellow, he can't enjoy it himself. But the best thing about the place was Miss Dormer—Reginald's sister : you know she's there as——"

" Yes—yes—I know."

" It made my heart ache to see her there ; though they behave admirably to her, and she seems quite contented. But for all that, she must feel it. I tell you what, old fellow ! if I could afford and could make up my mind to marry, she is just the girl I should like."

"She would make anybody an excellent wife, there's no doubt of it. But of course you can afford it. Why, you have 550*l.* a-year of your own, and then there's your pay. Of course I mean you could afford to marry *her*, brought up in her quiet way."

"No—no—I couldn't : not, at least, till I got my step ; and even then, it would be hard work to make both ends meet. And—bah ! —I have no right to think of marrying any-body. Besides, I am quite sure, if she accepted me, that she would make me leave the army. She was very kind to me ; but then she knew I was your friend."

" I don't see why that should interest her very much in you. . . . Hey ! cabby ! pull up —that's it."

They *were* rather late ; the rooms were crowded ; and Vavasour was glad to engage himself straightway to one of Morley's sisters.

" How fortunate to meet you at once ! I have only just arrived. You are not engaged for this waltz ? No, you must not be." And he bore her away.

" You have only just come. Then you have not seen Frank, or Mr. Dormer ? "

" No ; neither."

" They are both here. We should have liked Miss Dormer to have come with us so much, but she could not on account of her mourning. Do you know we are in such grief ; she is going to leave us."

" To leave you ! Why, she has not been with you a couple of months, has she ? "

" Not quite two months yet. The fact is—

but if I tell you, you must not tell anybody—
anybody, mind—mamma began to be afraid that
she and Frank were getting fond of each other ;
she certainly was very attentive to my brother.
And though you know she is quite a lady in
every way, yet she would scarcely be suitable
for Frank ; there is a distinction between them,
after all. Well, mamma thought it better to
guard against the danger, and very kindly told
her that she wished to be frank with her, and
that she feared that her youth exposed her to
what might ultimately cause her own unhappiness, as well as that of others ; and that as soon
as she could meet with a home, mamma thought
she had better accept it. Now I know I ought
not to have told you, but you will not mention
it, will you? and, of all people, not to
Frank."

" Certainly not."

" It turns out very fortunately that her
grandpapa, Mr. Chesterfield, wants her to live
with him. He wanted her to do so at first,
shortly after her papa's death, but she would
not. But as he positively refuses—at least I

have heard this—to assist her brother in his profession as an artist, if she will not, she has consented, particularly after what mamma said to her. I fancy he is a queer man, her grand-papa ; he disapproved of her mother marrying Mr. Dormer, and never would have anything to say to them ; but now that only these two young people are left, and he is himself a widower, I suppose he is glad to have Miss Dormer with him,"

Why did Vavasour insist that Miss Morley should dance the next quadrille with him ? Why did he pour into her ear flatteries as stupidly fulsome as any uttered that night, except that they were more skilful ? Why did he avail himself of the opportunities of the dance to toy with the frail fingers of that gossiping doll ? Why did he fling into his glance a fond interest, that was only less wonderful if feigned than it had been wonder-ful if felt ? And why did he beg, ay, and get, the choicest lily from her nosegay, as they stood screened in the verandahed window ? A moment after, when he had left her side, he

had crushed it in his hand, and with a curse,
flung it into the street.

"Ah, Miss Latimer. Your card, your card ;
is it very full ? "

" You do not deserve to find a vacant dance,
after coming so late, and then dawdling through
a waltz and a quadrille with Miss Morley."

" Shall I go away then, with my deserts ? "

She gave him her card, and her arm.

" I have had great trouble, I assure you, to
keep myself disengaged. What is this new
idea of yours ? I lose your identity, when I
see you bring pleasant blushes into the blonde
cheek of Adelaide Morley."

" May I not sit under shady trees as well as
my neighbours ? You know there is an Arabian
tree famed for its courtesy, that bends down its
branches to every comer ; there are a great
many courteous trees here that ought to be
famous. But why may not Adelaide Morley
blush as well as her betters ? Women avenge
themselves for their generosity towards us by
their uncompromising selfishness towards each
other."

o

"Nay, I am unconcerned about what Miss Morley may do; I do not think she has any identity. But you have; and I do not like you to lose it."

"Do I recover it now?" he asked, and slightly pressed against his the rounded arm he held. Simply, but with a strangely sweet and soft prolongation of the sound that writing cannot represent, she answered:

"Yes."

They had waltzed, and were stepping into the balcony.

"I fear you have not suffered enough to be happy," Varasour was saying.

"Ah!" she answered, "if suffering will bring happiness, I must be reaching the promised land."

The early night had glistened with constellations; but the huntress of the sky had come, had chased the stars, and shone in the triumph of her solitude. Subduedly came the music to their ears; subduedly the circular rush of faithful feet. He bent down and felt for the fragrance of her flowers. They lay, as did her hand which held them, across his arm. Was it the intoxication of those rich exotics that led his hand to hers?

" Never mind, Blanche ; we must try if we cannot both be happy."

What did he mean ? Had any one dared to ask him, he would have certainly answered :

" Nothing."

But as if he had said too much, he exclaimed immediately :

" Weariness is only another word, invented by self-love, for dulness. But human happiness, like human truth, is never more than fractional. Youth, with its capacities for love, is denied the one thing—money—which justifies its indulgence ; and money pours in when the plenitude of the passions has departed. Yet he who thinks himself more miserable, will soon come to think himself more virtuous than his neighbours, and it needs but these two convictions to equip an accomplished egotist. Come, let us go and prove that *we* are not egotists."

And he led her again into the crowd.

Where are we ? Music still : lights still :

dancing still : but assuredly this is not Chesham Place. I see Morley, Grafton, Reginald, but not Adelaide, nor Blanche, or if such, supposititious ones. I recognise the faces of the aristocracy of the unrecognised, and—is it so ? look again—yes, I see Vavasour. I think we had better go away, even though we leave him there.

CHAPTER IX.

WITH no premonitory coyness, but with a single bound, spring had burst upon the land and turned us all glad. Yet it is perhaps at such a period, more than any other, that the thoughtful among us are harried by vagrant regrets, especially if we, unlike the year, have no new livery to don ; if to us, less fortunate than external nature, there have come no second creation.

There might have been perceived in Vavasour about this time a discontent and fretfulness, which no sarcastic optimism could hide. He had become more skilled in reporting, and had so increased his income ; but he talked like a man who has failed and would not have anyone know it. This frame of mind, however, or at least its outward show, passed away ; and by

the middle of May he was apparently on as
good terms with himself and others as before.
But whether proclaiming arrogantly that life is
a luxury to every man that has a decent palate,
or implying through the plaintive medium of
sardonic accusation that there are some men
for whom the world is not good enough—in
either mood, and indeed in other moods (if
there were such) he seemed still more and
more, since Lady Harbledown yet continued in
Italy, gravitating towards the society of Blanche
Latimer. Always comprehending him, she appeared to like his clouded humours only just
less than his sunny ones. At least, she either
appreciated or over-rated his abilities ; and in
either case he was not likely to find much fault.
The least skilful woman, and she was scarcely
that, can always reach the stronghold of the
most skilful man (and he had as little claim to
the one character as she had to the other)
through the avenues of his vanity. I make the
remark generally, and indeed rather imperti-
nently, since I think it has no very great
reference to them. Yet though she might not

harbour the intention of using *as a weapon* that most delicate of all flatteries, appreciation, it is certain that she used it, and that it had its effect. Is it wonderful that he had come to say frequently to himself, " There's no one like Blanche," and to carry his belief up to a certain point into practice ?

But though it may be very agreeable, and even the limit of ambition, to a young man to be understood, more especially by a young, handsome, and admired girl, it is a little unreasonable to expect that she should find full remuneration in the mere consciousness of understanding him. And men, even egotistical young men of twenty-five, are not all metaphysics. Even they have an illogical knack of sometimes clinching a loose argument with a squeeze of the hand, and carrying conviction, when all else has failed, by a skilful, illicit distribution of the middle of the sofa. And so though, on walking Templewards after one of those evenings in which most heterodox ideas, most classical music, and sentimental passages-of-arms had divided the hours, it might be very gratifying to Vavasour to swing his umbrella, walk erect, and swear there was no one like Blanche ; did it ever occur to him to inquire if Blanche might have come to think that there was no one like Mr. Vavasour ? There is a conceit so concentrated that a man possessed by it will actually cease to ask himself what impression he creates upon his neighbours.

Vavasour had been to the first Flower Show of the season, had been dining with Mr. Latimer, and was now walking with Blanche (some other of her visitors at no great distance) up and down the private garden enclosures of Regent's Park.

"Ah, no," he was saying to her ; " suffering is the only thing that makes women faithful."

" Then how do you account for men winning women by their tenderness ? "

" I spoke of 'securing,' not of 'winning.' But even taking your modified way of putting it, I account for it by denying it. The way to make a woman love you is to show her that you love —not her, but—yourself. You would cease to care for me if you thought I cared for you better than I care for myself."

"Mr. Vavasour!" She stopped suddenly, both in her speech and in her walking. He turned to her.

"*Eh bien?*"

They walked on as before. She spoke rapidly.

"You are always saying things like what you have said just now, and then turning away with a laugh that is not pleasant. The question arises, not whether you care for yourself better than for me, but whether you care for me at all. I have no mother; papa troubles himself little about me. I am not a mere girl; if I do not ask you the question, no one else will." He brushed the grass lazily with his feet as he walked by her side, raised his eyebrows—perhaps even a little his shoulders—but said nothing.

"*Do* you care for me?"

"It is not a good time to ask the question," he said at length; "for twilight changes and confuses the colour of our feelings no less strikingly than of our flowers or our dresses."

"But the question *is* asked : to put it once is painful enough ; to have to put it a second time would be intolerable, perhaps impossible."

"I think you might have discovered that I do not care much for anybody or anything. You know I profess to be very tolerant ; but toleration is only thrown in when by pain one purchases indifference. *I* have made my bargain. Is it necessary to show you still more than I have already shown you all along, that I am an acceptor of facts and circumstances ? that I have arrived at that stage when a man considers that to be best which is most readily got and most easily retained ? Prove to me that a thing is impossible, and I cease to regard it as desirable. Really, I want nothing ; unless it be the privilege to live and to laugh. There are many difficulties in life : argument leaves them where it found them ; reflection only aggravates the entanglement ; a laugh or a paradox will solve them all."

"And you think this an answer ? You say you want nothing ; why, your conduct—your life—is a constant aggression. There is no

design so deep as the design of indifference.
But are you indifferent? not in your behaviour,
surely. You treat me as though you were playing a game : you fling out the ball sometimes,
but only, before the cord snaps, to pull it back
again suddenly and catch it. You will not let
it go, nor let it rest. I know that cleverness
will often induce the feeling of scorn, and to that
extent I understand you ; but that you, you at
your age should—I will not say boast of, lament
(if you like)—that you should lament being
the victim of indifference, this I cannot understand ? "

"How should you ? I have known you two
years now, have seen much of you ; what do we
know of each other ? Our real sorrows are the
sorrows we never mention ; you may be quite
sure I have never mentioned mine, though you
are scarcely dull enough to suppose that I have
not had any. I would willingly, like that sheet
of water there, give back from my surface the
pleasant twilight hues, and say nothing about
any fetid matter that may be rotting or rotten
deeper down ; but you drag me. Do not then

complain of what you haul up. I can remember
well enough—I will not say how long ago—
writing in answer to the expressed alarm that
time and distance, and in fact life generally
might modify my then unfolded passion, writing
(and for aught I know the writing exists at this
day) the wonderful words, 'my darling, my
darling! it is impossible.' Well, the then impossible is the now actual, and—why, we are
walking here: that is the answer to it. Through
the pitiful veil of a wretchedly-hung timidity, I
did not then see—fool that I was not to see! I
see it now—the love that would have leaped up
wildly to six hundred a-year." It had come to
this, had it? This was how he spoke of Mary
Dor——nay, let him go on. "It needed but a
freak of finance to bring her heart throbbing
where, by God's truth, it shall never throb. Bah!
I raved—and am laughing. Do you want galvanised lees? My love-cup has long since ceased
to sparkle. I have seen vulgar people dip bread
into the wine from which genuine effervescence
had departed, and so create a make-believe
effervescence. No household bread, no home

leaven, be sure, will do for me even that baby's
office. The lees must be galvanised, I say;
your hand would soon tire of working the
battery."

" I think," she said, " we had better leave the
past alone. Nothing so wonderful to a woman
—I suppose it is the same with men—as her
past, if she have the courage, I had better say
the vulgar folly, to look at it. You drag your
heart—not I; but you neither surprise nor
disenchant me. I have met girls who made
much boast of their discovery that the boy who
loved them had never loved before; I could
never see the grounds of their self-congratu-
lation. To love one person after having loved
another is (if one would only be philosophical,
and *you* would have us all so) a poorer compliment, it seems to me, to the first love than to
the second—the second has no cause to complain, the first very soon will have. We are
inductive animals, as I have heard you say;
and one experiment is not enough to satisfy
us."

With a most indecent haste and unseemly

interruption—an interruption, though, which he could not resist, he exclaimed delightedly :

"Excellent, excellent! What good things you say! You leave me behind. I must remember all that." As though they discussed an abstract proposition, and he were personally altogether unconcerned! She could scarcely fail to notice, but bore with it.

"But to say," she continued, "that faith once disappointed, or love once unreturned"——

"Scarcely that, Blanche! If my love had not been returned, be sure I never should have told you of it. Nothing so much prevents a man's success with one woman as her knowledge that he has failed with another ; prestige carries many otherwise impregnable positions."

How patient she was with him!

"I did not wish to assume that your love had ever been unreturned, though to suppose that impossible is to think higher of my sex than my experience will allow me. But what does it amount to ? You believed once what you do not believe now, and so you will never believe again."

"Even so : I suffer from a passive incredulity. I do not believe in any one ; I do not believe in you ; but most of all I do not believe in the person in whom I once had the most implicit credence—myself. The 'my darling, my darling, it is impossible ;' looks at me from the page of the past and grins at me ; a very devil's grin would it be, could I too not grin back. A strain of music, a warm sundown, beautiful hair when with one's hand one smooths it—these bring a transitory faith. Do you wish me to believe in these ? Will you lean on such a rotten reed as that ? I *have* heard music, I *have* watched sunsets, I *have* smoothed tresses, which have excited in me the delirious desire to be the Alexander, the Xavier, the Abelard, of my age ; the next evening has found me in the reporters' gallery. A fair share of imagination will land a man for five minutes anywhere he likes ; it requires something very different to keep him for fifty years faithfully anchored to the fire-irons. The human nature which either education or accident has not reduced to the requisite state of submission, will soon rebel against the slavery of slippers. I am more rebellious by accident even than by character, and the luckiest moment of my life was when, though I swore to my darling that change was impossible, my darling did not believe me."

" Your whole moral," she answered, with a retributive logic that far surpassed his own, " is that all feelings are more or less transitory; and yet the whole strength of your position depends upon the assumption that your present feelings—or perhaps I should say, absence of feelings—will be permanent. Clearly, it is not a matter of argument, when you argue so badly. Be it so. But mind, I will not lose you as a friend; only I would ask you to try and be more consistently and equably platonic. If you are not deceiving yourself, and the description of your feelings be a faithful one, there is one thing at least which I do not envy you. Do not take away from me entirely, as I fear you have already taken partially, the only possession in which I am more gifted than you are. Leave me what little faith you have not altogether sapped to-night ; for a woman cannot afford to be a sceptic in the creed of the heart."

I do not know if she really tried to speak the concluding words with firmness ; if she tried, she failed. The halting utterance, the tremulous tones, pierced through the deepening dusk, and told to Vavasour the troubled tale of tears. The serenest scorn that ever sat upon the lip of women can be met with scorn at least as serene ; the most collected coldness with which she thinks to guard her garrison can be starved out with a coldness even better supplied ; her smiles bestowed upon a rival can be successfully encountered by your smiles bestowed upon yourself. Bah ! she will beat you still. She will weep, and you shall surrender. Artist, take from me a hint, and mould me your Venus Victrix—in tears. He stretched his arm athwart her, and patted rather than pressed her shrinking shoulder.

"They say, Blanche, that men are never re-converted ; try you to show that they are wrong. See, they are coming towards us ; indeed it is time to go."

P

It was ; for the twilight had all but melted into the monarchy of night. They walked homewards ; Vavasour talked gaily with everybody, everybody but with Blanche. She went to the piano in the back drawing-room, and sang Mercadante's "Soave Imagine." He went to her as it drew to a close.

"I am going ; good night." She gave her hand, but still sat before the instrument. He bent slowly down and kissed her forehead. "Have faith ; it depends on you whether I shall recover it. After all, it is affectation for any one to pretend to be altogether an indifferent : life is a game in which everybody has a part mapped out, and so nobody can be umpire."

"Are you going to the Greshams' on the 2nd ? " asked Mr. Latimer, as Vavasour made his adieux. "Well then, dine with us, and we will give you a seat."

Vavasour thanked him, and departed. Does any one—nay, do many, think that between his frequent guest and his daughter, a most strange liberality of intercourse was permitted? Doubtless, a mother would have stopped this skirmishing long ago, but fathers are less skilful in bringing love engagements to close quarters. Besides, Mr. Latimer feared his daughter as much on thirty days of the month, as he made her fear him on the thirty-first. By abusing her once a month, and losing his temper once a day, he thought he had fully asserted his parental authority and fulfilled his paternal responsibility.

He had every reason to suppose that Vavasour would not marry for seven or eight years [to come, and none to suppose that he would ever marry his daughter. Indeed he considered Blanche quite set apart for his friend in India. He liked Vavasour, though he did not quite like his insolent way of going on. He sneered at him to Blanche one day, and asked him to dinner the next. So that who can say he did not make very handsome reparation ?

* * * * * *

" No more wine, Mr. Vavasour ?—just a glass of sherry. Very well. If you will go up to the drawing-room, I will be there directly ; the carriage ought to be round."

He went up-stairs and lolled on the sofa ; no one was in the drawing-room ; but presently Blanche came in, with a halo of gossamer and smiles.

" Admire me, sir, instead of lolling there. Am I nice ? Am I horrid ? What am I ? "

He stretched out his hands ; she thought it was in order to be raised up, and so gave hers. But he drew her towards him.

" You are charming, my dear." She drew back from the calculated salute. " As you will," he said with an unruffled countenance, and let go her hands. " But it is scarcely wise to refuse what so many are ready to grant."

" I know best about that," she replied ; and Mr. Latimer entered.

One of the boys completed the quartet. Vavasour discussed vintages with Mr. Latimer the whole way. He danced his first dance with Blanche, but was most cheerfully distant, said the dullest things in the liveliest manner with supreme unconsciousness, and left her to go and speak to Stephen Grafton.

"She's here, with her grandfather ; I am going to dance this next quadrille with her."

" My good fellow ; *who* is here ? What are you talking about in that excited manner? Calm yourself ; I really do not understand you."

" Of course you do. Miss Dormer is here, with old Chesterfield ; very handsome old boy, but battered."

"Oh, *she* is here, is she ? Now you grow intelligible. And you dance this quadrille with her ? Yes, I see her ; I must go and pay my respects."

And he walked over to where she sat, in half mourning still, next to Mr. Chesterfield. She introduced him. A few words were spoken ; might he have the honour of dancing that quadrille with her ? She was *very* sorry, she was engaged for *that* dance to Mr. Grafton. He bowed and retired.

A ball-room in full motion faithfully photographed, would be a greater triumph even than the scudding clouds, or the scampering tide similarly rendered. These have been done; can that? Leech has often drawn it, and always failed. He need not be annoyed. It is beyond his art, not him. A pen is a clumsier weapon than a pencil, and, in the unskilled hand that holds this, the result would be a caricature that would not even be comic. I forbear, and follow the hours. It is after supper.

"Mr. Vavasour," eagerly whispered a voice on the landing, as he was about to re-enter the ball-room. He looked; it was Miss Dormer.

"Pardon me! Yes?"

"Mr. Chesterfield has gone. I fear I was long in looking for my cloak, and he has gone— without me. He is odd sometimes, and does strange things."

"And you wish to go, of course? and you want a cab? and——"

"And I do not want it to be noticed." Her lashes closed over her eyes and opened again in the old way. (He wished she would not do it!) "I can ask no one here so well as —as you. Will you be good enough to take.

me home and hide—what has happened? It
is very humiliating. You see, Reginald is
not here."

He did it as well as it could be done : and
their exit was screened, I fancy, from at least
all but straggling servants in the hall and the
porch.

" I am so sorry to give you this trouble,"
she said, as the cab drove off ; " it is very kind
of you. I am subject occasionally to these
peculiarities of grandpapa's ; but he is very
good to me—and to Reginald."

" Yes, yes. Old men of course are whimsical, lose their tempers and their — grand-
children : but there's nothing in it. The
vagaries of the old are the amusements of
the young : they should never be taken *au
grand sérieux.*"

The cab was driven at full speed.

" Are you very busy, Mr. Vavasour ? Are
you writing anything—any—any Poem ? "

" Oh, dear no ! " and he laughed. " I have
long since seen the necessity of surrendering
ill-chosen and ill-fortified opinions. Poets are

but a better sort of acrobats. With great
difficulty they learn to fling themselves into unnatural contortions, and to mount unsteady and
altogether unnecessary ladders. The attempt
is dangerous ; the attainment not very digni-
fied. If they succeed, they get more plaudits
than pence ; if they fail, they break their
heads—their hearts, I have heard, but I dis-
believe that. Excellent dance! was it not ? "

" Very : yes—very."

" Is this your street ? "

" No ; the next."

" Very pleasant neigbourhood. No place
like London : is there ? "

" I cannot say I am very fond of it. It is
a large heartless place."

" Perhaps it is : but I am not sure that is
not its chief recommendation. If it gives
nothing, it asks nothing : it is not generous,
but any rate it is not exacting. Ha! we are
here."

" I am so——"

" Oh, no ; not at all : very glad to be of
service." The hall-door did not close upon her

before she had caught the words : "Back to Mr. Gresham's, cabby! and as quickly as you can."

Mr. Chesterfield had not shown much kindness in leaving Miss Dormer behind: he showed even less in his reception of her on her arrival ; but for all that, I scarcely think that this combined cruelty and coarseness quite account for that flood of tears which the poor girl sheds on reaching her solitary bed-chamber, whose door, with your permission, I will draw gently to.

    *   *   *   *   *

" I thought you had gone : you were engaged to me for the lancers : and they are over."

" Never mind : this galop instead."

" I must go after that. Papa has gone, he was very tired, but my brother is here."

Vavasour would accept a "lift" in their carriage : the brother wanted to smoke and would ride outside. Excellent brother !

" You have behaved very strangely to-night."

" Have I ? I thought I had never been so amiable. I have just been compensating my-

self for your protective customs by the most
unrestrained approach of—nay, I must not tell
you whom.   But then it was after supper; and
champagne is the Cobden of society : the real
repealer of duties."

He laughed and he bantered; and he
gossipped—about everybody but her : he quite
forgot the lover's rule to speak of no one save
"*d'elle et de moi.*"   She felt cross, and looked
feverish, but could not make him serious.   At
last she brightened up, and said cheerfully :

" You are very unforgiving : but remember
that I too have had—champagne."

Her meaning was not very obscure; but
obscure or significant, he was not likely to
miss it.   He drew her gently towards him,
she assisted now, rather than repelled him.
His arm was round her waist : his hands held
hers; her cheek rested upon his — rounded
damask peach against a hothouse wall.

It was difficult to decide, no doubt.   There
was but one arrow left in the quiver; and
manifestly every other had failed of its mark.
Should this fall short or fly over, the armoury

was empty! Ought she to have reserved it
still? She thought otherwise, and has aimed:
has this last shaft hit or missed the target of
his heart? We must follow up and see.

Letters are the sand-banks of love: yet
where are the betrothed who are wise enough
to eschew them? If one note seem not un-
satisfactory—not short of the affection due—
to him or her who receives it, the next is sure
to seem so, unless it surpass in fond inuendoes
or epithets the extravagance of its predecessor.
The deep must have a deeper still, or will soon
begin to appear very shallow: so that this
correspondence has to become an arithmetical
progression, *ad infinitum*, which has neither
extremes nor mean. Practically, this is impossible. Then come complaints, taunts, regrets,
accusations of coldness, rebukes of "you do
not write as you wrote at first,"—nay, who
does not know it?

. Does this not account for the silly love-letters
which even clever people write, and for the
cleverest people refusing to write them at all?
Common-place correspondents can get over

half a dozen, nay, half a million, quarrels as easily as they can get over writing or reading erotic rubbish : but better minds will not long submit to the degradation of either. An argument disenchants, a cold letter alienates, a warm letter disgusts, them : they turn from those passionate paroxysms of the pen which only display and still further weaken self-indulgent natures. But they are the men whom women will persist in loving, to their cost. They are the men, say you, who do not love at all. Well, they are: yet blame them not ; they can discover their inability to love only by trying.

Vavasour tried : and the postman was at his door oftener than heretofore. But if he had acquired the habit of speaking curtly, he wrote even more so ; and never so strikingly as in answer to an affectionate letter. If, as though by an intentional change of tactics, there came one cool and cautious, he did not, unless the contents absolutely demanded, an-swer it at all ; but would meet her, who had written it, a few days after, with a cheerful indifference which she could not fail to see was altogether unfeigned.

"I fancy I should make a very decent husband," he would say, "but I shall never know how to play the part of lover. I see no prospect of ever being the former: and I have nothing—I never shall have anything; I am not a money-making animal. As I have told you all along, Blanche, you are very foolish. Look at Morley: those are the men. Now that his father is dead, he must have three thousand a-year."

"I do not see what Mr. Morley has to do with it. Are you really leaving town on the 30th?" It was July.

"No doubt of it."

"You will only write when I tell you that you may: and I must always address to your chambers, and they will be forwarded?"

"Exactly."

Nothing is to me so great a trial of patience as to have to read the correspondence of other people: I conclude your tastes to be similar, and so forbear from producing even extracts from theirs. It was not, I am bound to say, an unmeritorious correspondence : it really had some very good literary points, and even some quick glimpes into human nature. Instructive it certainly would be : sometimes, perhaps, entertaining ; but, for all, I abstain. Sufficient let it be to chronicle its existence.

It was the evening of the 29th of July. Vavasour had packed up : early in the morning he should leave Town, and these last hours were to be spent with Stephen Grafton, at the Club of the latter. It was time to go. There was a postman's knock.

" Stephen's writing, surely ? "

" Don't come this evening, old boy," the letter ran, " I could not bear it ; you can guess why. There is talk to-day at the Horse-Guards of our regiment going to Canada. In my bitter disappointment, I almost hail this news as a relief.

" Yours affectionately,

" STEPHEN GRAFTON."

" So Mary has refused him. Poor fellow !

If he only knew that she has done the same to me. It is idle to pretend to myself that I am sorry, on the whole, though I regret that dear old Stephen should suffer. I suppose I must do as he wishes, and not go to him. Well, I will finish my book and send it back to the Library. And to-morrow for North Wales and some fresh air.

CHAPTER X.

IF you want to discover how you can spend three months, and yet have nothing to say about them except that they were "very jolly," go and shoot or fish for twelve consecutive weeks in a hilly country. This had Cyril been doing, and now found himself again before a blazing fire in his Temple chambers, and a heap of letters before him. "From Blacklock. An age since I saw him. Will come to see me to-morrow night, at half-past eleven. Delighted to see him. Bill. Another. Circular. Dun. Stephen : regiment definitely ordered abroad. Well, let all go. Foreign letters. Yes, by Jove! from Lady Harbledown. Coming home : will be in town by the 20th of October. That's to-day. Bravo! And now for this one."

"This one," as he called it, was from Blanche

Latimer. It had caught his eye at first; but he had allowed it to remain to the last.

Probably the solitude of the mountains had softened his heart, and he had begun to yearn for peace—peace on any terms. Besides, he was becoming more open to conviction that it was to be found in domestic life, even when attended with some denials. And so, I fancy, had it come to pass that he had about six weeks back written Blanche a letter—long, affectionate, and yearning: the fondest letter he had ever sent her. A week later came one from her—short, cold, indifferent—such indeed as he had never yet received. It consisted chiefly of gossip about Reginald. He did not answer it, feeling indeed annoyed at having written his last long effusion. Doubtless—so he chose to think— she fancies that her triumph has come; that she has made me love her deeply at last, and will in turn try the power of prolonged indifference. Fool, not to know me better! when I have myself told her that I like best what is most readily got and most easily retained! So he did not write, nor did she. Not till now, at

Q

least, after a five weeks' silence. A letter from
her lay before him. He opened it now. It
was plaintive and conciliatory, accusing him of
his harsh neglect, and asking if he intended to
write to her again.

He sat down, and wrote rapidly,

"MY DEAR MISS LATIMER,

"I have a strong partiality for feeling
that I am right; none for proving it. When a
man has convinced himself, he may be quite sure
that he has completed his list of converts.

"There are men whom no tenderness can win,
whom no logic can convince, but who can be
outwitted like sheep. I am of a different type.
An argument will satisfy, a spontaneous kiss will
persuade, me; but stratagems only keep my head
on the alert, and only induce me to still further
strengthen the approaches to my heart.

"Believe me, with great respect, yours sincerely,
                              "CYRIL VAVASOUR."

"If that does not bring to a conclusion this
detestable affair, what will? The girl but

wastes my time, and does not help me to either happiness or advancement. But she has been, like Tennyson's Juliet—

> ' The summer pilot of an empty heart
> Unto the shores of Nothing ——'

and so valuable. Summer is over, and—what care I ? To-morrow for Lady Harbledown."

If people will go away and leave us behind, they must accept the consequences of their absence. They return, and accuse us of infidelity ; we wept over their departure, and do not weep over their arrival, only because we have long since ceased to weep at all. They went, and left a complete vacuum ; they come back, and we cannot find them one vacant place. Friends, once separated, should never meet again. Men continue to believe in the illusions of their youth, because they are at a distance ; come face to face with them, and they are as dull as the dinner of to-day.

Cyril Vavasour seeks Lady Harbledown. Two years have intervened since their hands pressed good-bye. You know if *he* has changed. Query, has she ? The matrimonial state is not favourable to mental growth : the progressive minds are the unattached. Will she rally him now ? He will yawn. She left an impulsive boy : she will find a measured man. A believing enthusiast provoked her kindly banter : the faith that never wholly leaves a woman will evoke the smile of the sceptic. Why, he has become the very thing he scorned ; the incarnation of what his boyhood so indignantly denounced. It is well to tolerate the views of our neighbours, if for no other motive, at least for this, that in condemning theirs we may beforehand be condemning our own. The man who is sure that any one thing is altogether right, and its opposite altogether wrong, is easily convinced.

Was she as beautiful as ever ? That was, I believe, the question he put most anxiously as he sat awaiting her. It is the question of questions, after all. We grow sentimental over ruined abbeys, dismantled castles, green court-yards, weed-grown graves ; but to me the ruins of a bygone beauty are the mournfullest ruins of all. History is eloquently moral over empires lost ; but thousands of sceptres slip away from the hands that grasped them gracefully, and no one tells ; *la reine est morte—vive la reine!* Belisarius on a doorstep, Bajazet in a cage, Napoleon on a wave-washed boulder, have not half the pathos of that unsolicited, supperless wallflower, who was once the petitioned of the ball-room and the toast of the wine-flask.

No, she is beautiful still. Mabel, Lady Harbledown need not mourn as yet over the ravages of Time the Visigoth. She has been in the land of loveliness, and she seems to have borrowed of its charms, and so to have enhanced her own. But the brilliancy of its sun has not scattered from its face the melancholy that we have all come to regard as the appanage of Italy ; and this gift, amongst the rest, it struck Vavasour, had, since their separation, fallen to the lot of her who now stood before him.

However much we are to disagree or dislike each other afterwards, our greetings are always cordial : such was theirs. But why, he wondered, did tears flood her eyes as their hands met, and remain there, and even mount anew ever and anon, as they spoke of the lengthened interval which neither had expected? Hers had never seemed a tearful nature; had they changed places in the lapsed period? The most skilled of us know not what to say the first time we come together again, provided we are glad at the reunion. Vavasour had felt this before; but still, the difficulty of conversation, and the constraint which increased as the evening wore on, were not accounted for. They were alone, yet they were not garrulous. She did not question him as of old : perhaps she saw there was too much to tell, and perhaps some of that much which she should not like to hear. She guessed his growth at a glance, but shrank from taking its exact proportions ; nor was he communicative as to his development. Would she sing to him? she must have sung in Italy. She had never made pretensions to great skill; but she had truth and taste. She sang; she wavered—trembled—paused—and was again in tears.

"I am so nervous, Mr. Vavasour! you must pardon me. I have not been strong in Italy, and my weakness shows itself in this stupid manner."

And in that stupid manner did it show itself again more than once : tears that never trespassed beyond the eye, or beyond the tone, but never quite abandoned either. Vavasour lingered, hoping that Sir Wilfrid would make his appearance. Yes, she hoped he would come soon : she did not know where he was, but he could not be long. However, he did not come, and Vavasour remembered Blacklock's promised visit. He was very sorry not to see Sir Wilfrid, but must go : he should soon come again, and drive away the nervousness. When had he spent so downcast an evening? Was this Mabel?

He hurried on homewards. When he was about the middle of the Strand, he found the causeway blocked up by a collection of people, which, as is usual in London, gathered and gathered still.

" Take her up, can't you ? "

" Shame ! shame ! "

" She's dying ! "

"Dying! she's drunk, that's all."

"Now then; what's it all about?"

"Only a woman."

"Carry her somewhere."

"Carry her yourself."

"I'm sure she's dying."

"And I'm sure she's drunk."

"She is neither drunk nor dying," said Vavasour, taking her arm as she lay on the step; "she is dead."

"Dead?"

"Dead; not a doubt of it."

A couple of policemen came.

"Yes, she is dead."

And they lifted up the corpse.

Vavasour still gazed upon the face whose features had at first so attracted him. He had seen them somewhere, he was sure. It was no use following them any further. He had stared at them till he could carry them away in his eye without more external aid. He walked on, puzzling his memory; he could make nothing of it beyond this, that the face of the dead woman was not new to him.

"Here just before me." Blacklock stood at the outer door. "Hope I have not kept you waiting; I thought I was never going to see you again. Have you ever called since last December?"

"No, never; last December, was it? Yes, nearly a year ago."

"Hah! an excellent fire, with a poke or two. Take the arm-chair; I am delighted to see you."

"And I, you. What about the 'Book?'"

"The 'Book?' Oh, yes! the 'Book.' Still-born, sir, like the paradoxes mentioned in the 'Vicar of Wakefield;' the world said nothing to my 'Book,' absolutely nothing. The reviews never noticed it, not one of them."

"I hope you feel the compliment. If they could have ridiculed you, they would, depend on it; it was not likely they were going to help you to ridicule themselves. Then there is an end of it?"

"A complete end of it; I had forgotten all about it, though it cost me some 35*l*., a sum I could not well afford."

"Never mind. I often think that the fertility of some men is owing to the amount of dirt they had to eat in their youth. Swallow yours contentedly. We should do with our dead projects, our failures, as gardeners do with dead leaves—use them for manure."

"Well; but you surely have come to London for some time? I have missed no one so much as you; you must come oftener."

"Truth to tell, I have come to say good-bye to you for the last time."

"How so? Do you leave England?"

"Yes, Europe. Like Ulysses,

'my purpose holds
To sail beyond the sunset;'

and you are the only man I shall take the trouble to part with. You will never see me again; you have behaved kindly to me, and I have faith in your future—probably you have yourself. I am not an egotist, that you must have seen; but a sketch of my history may prove of use to you, and so you shall have it. You are the one person I have met who never manifested an indecent, ill-bred curiosity; you are the one person who will derive the slightest real benefit from the knowledge of my career."

Vavasour confessed that he had ever felt the curiosity, which he had always concealed.

"No doubt; it shall be gratified. My misfortunes commenced early; my first misfortune was to be born a gentleman, and an eldest—nay, an only—son, and from that misfortune I have never recovered. As if I had not been sufficiently ill-treated, I grew up both good-looking and clever; and my people knew and cared for it more even than I knew and cared for it myself. I have what is called good blood in my veins; the man who seriously dwells on such a fiction is a self-condemned fool. I mention it in order to be understood. If I am not, and was not then, proud of my parentage, others were; and looked to me as the restorer of a race which had certainly become rather in want of renovation. I heard much of estates that had passed away—I never saw them; I saw only a decent manor recently purchased, and not even entailed. I shone at school—the only place where shining is a pleasure—and

went to college. I gave suppers, but I studied
too ; and I don't care saying that I felt—it was
well enough known and acknowledged then—
that I should leave the University a double-
first, the terror of bargemen, and the most
popular fellow of my time. I left it none of
the three, for I left it shrouded in a mystery
which I well know has never been solved.
When a man says he loves a woman, to praise
her is mere pleonasm; and no one will agree
with him, except by also loving her—a result
not desired. When I say that I loved the
daughter of a miller (her father was dead),
I have told you as much as you would care to
know." He took a great long breath, and his
huge chest expanded like a blacksmith's bellows.
His pipe was out ; he lit it again, and went on.
" One hears random talk of seduction. If by
seduction you mean the cautious use of measured means which, like the machinery for all
desired results, will generally accomplish its
purposes, I did not——" He slackened speed
in his swift speech, as though he answered an
accuser,—" I did not seduce that poor child. I

determined she should be my wife ; but I would
gain my college honours first. With these in
one hand, I could, with better grace and better
hope of acceptance, lead the miller's daughter
to my people's presence with the other. I do
not know through whose kind intervention—
thank Heaven ! I do not know, or I should have
sent him to be judged there long ago—my
connection with her became known at my
home, even though it was not known at hers.
But a few weeks before my examination, I
received a pressing summons home. I went.
Frankly my father charged me ; frankly I
confessed. How far had the affair gone ? I
told him. He did not say it was wicked ; he
said it was unfortunate, but he would help me
out of it. The girl's mother was sure to discover it : he would himself tell her, and make
all necessary arrangements—money arrangements, of course, with which they would be
satisfied, and I must not be such a fool again.
At once I spoke my secret resolve : I said I
would listen to no such proposal, I had all along
intended to marry, and only waited till I could

do so with better grace and with less offence. He stared; he swore; he threatened. I held my peace and showed my purpose. Well, he would think of it. He thought of it, and changed his mind. I might do as I would; it was an intolerable mortification to him, but he saw, he said, it was no using opposing me. At any rate, I should only have greater temptations to waste my time when near her than at home; and the next few weeks were precious. I worked hard, and then rushed up to college; when there, I hastened to her. Nor she, nor her mother, was where I left both; the place was deserted. They had left a fortnight before, without informing any-one of their intention: no one could answer my earnest inquiries further. Oh, fools! fools! We are educated to believe that it is always allowable to deceive children and women, par-ticularly for their own good; and I had deceived Nelly at least in this—that I had at first given her a name not my own, and had even gone so far as to represent myself resi-dent in London, and having no connection with the University. Day by day, though my love grew, did I put off undeceiving her; thinking only of the reparation I should shortly make. Doubtless she had, in my absence, written to the false name and the false address, and had at once her letter returned and her eyes opened. I hastened back home; my father affected surprise. I accused him bluntly of deceiving me. He shrugged his shoulders, and said she had, no doubt, gone away with a fool even greater than myself. He knew nothing; and if he did know, would tell nothing." He leaped to his feet. " There have been moments, Vavasour, when, had I met that man, I would have crushed him with my heel. By my soul's strength! this is one of them. He help me to marry her! he laughed in my face. That he had outwitted me he did not care to hide, but would not avow." He shook his great body, and flung back into the chair. " Words would not help you to understand what has followed, if you do not already comprehend it. I parted with my father at my father's door: he cursed me aloud—I cursed him in my

heart. I think both curses have, from all I
know, been answered. It is true my mother
was my mother, but she was his wife ; she did
not remain either very long. I had sisters ; I
talk of them as I think of them—as inanimate
objects. One had already quarrelled with her
father by marrying against his will ; the other
quarrelled with him shortly afterwards through
the husband, whom she had married against her
own. I do not know whether they live or not ;
I should scarcely know where to inquire, and
I have no desire to know." His tone had lost
all its savage bitterness : he spoke with a gay
carelessness. " What a life I have had of it ?
How well I remember coming to this big place !
At last I got to write and to be paid for
articles in a rascally monthly. The manager
of a theatre had swindled an author ; I penned
an indignant leader. My Editor could not
afford to insert it, he avowed, because he had
a free admission ! I have driven a cab ; I
have been a hair-dresser, and lost three situa-
tions from my incurable habit of brushing
puppies out of their chair ; I have been the

carver at a dining-room, and lost that post by
my reckless generosity,—the managers said I
should ruin them ; I have figured in *poses
plastiques*—in chalk and tights I have defied
the lightning many a time ; I have lived at a
toll-gate,—I liked that because I could read,
and could mulct everyone that passed. But
they put up what they call a chain-bar—you
must have seen them in the country—and so I
as often got tickets as toll. I could not stand
that, and I left. And then my existence since !
Oh, how pleasant, in an age which boasts of
being civilised, and surrounds itself with what
it calls sanctions, to sally from the stronghold
of one's poverty and nonentity, and make this
civilised world pay plentiful black-mail to the
savages whom it cannot altogether extirpate
Nay, you need not start ; I have never risked my
freedom much. You remember our first supper :
I have had many—given with a worse grace,
but given, for all that. I have travelled in
countries where to be hungry is to be fed ; but
I dislike voluntary charity. I would sooner
extort than accept. You are the only person

whose kindness is not an offence ; and I
made your acquaintance by swindling you.
Ha—ha ! Never mind. 'Tis a funny world—
the lost pleiad, as you say ; I think the other
six are as well without it." He commenced
walking about and singing snatches of a song.

"But your father—"

" Lives, I believe."

" But when he dies—"

" He will not leave his money to me ; but if
he did, I would open his grave and fling it in
after him. See—Vavasour ! you are a clever
fellow, and I think a deal of you : but I want
advice from nobody. I came here to give you
some."

" And it is—"

"This. Believe in yourself, and take Time
into partnership. Oh the misses we make by
impatience ! Time, so we will only let it, is
the complement of our shortcomings. It re-
trieves our blunders, redresses our wrongs,
solves our doubts, answers our questions, reads
our riddles, and even satisfies all our desires,
since it either fulfils or annihilates them. Do

you want to marry a maiden, the one marvel of the Universe? Well, you will live either to marry her or to thank God you didn't. Are you hungering after laurel-leaves? They shall encircle your brow, or you shall smile at the man whose brow they do. A kind sleeping partner, truly, this Time. No bill that he will not accept—none that he will not renew, and will let run as long as ever you like; with this proviso—mark you!—that you be not fool enough to discount the hour of triumph by self-flattering anticipation of applause. Never say, *this* shall succeed—*that* shall succeed; but ever, *I* shall succeed. Every failure is a step in advance; when you have discovered the difficulty, you have all but discovered the solution. Never accuse the world, for it is never wrong; never hastily transfer your former panegyrics of an occupation in which you are annoyed not to have succeeded, to a fresh occupation in which you have not yet failed ; for these are the petulances of a pestilent self-love. Do not be disenchanted because neither your neighbours nor yourself seems to grow wiser :

Bear, bear, bear! My idea of a philosopher is of one who feels and manifests perfect toleration of human nature. But above all, mistake not the one important condition of the age in which you are to act your part. If you will not understand the paramount necessity of putting yourself above money perplexities, the genius of all the archangels will not save you from dying in a ditch." Again, he said, " I know you will not scorn my short sermon ; I am twice your age nearly : my life has been a contemptible failure, and I am really anxious that yours should not be. Whatever good spirits there may be, protect you ! No, I would rather you stayed here." It was the first time he had ever offered his hand ; warmly he grasped Vavasour's, and departed.

CHAPTER XI.

IT was the debatable hour in the London streets between dayclose and the advent of the night. Some lamps were lit, some were not; curtains met your gaze from one house, blank windows from another.

A girl sat alone in a handsome room, with no light in it but the flicker of the fire and what might yet enter through the uncovered panes. She reclined in an easy chair; her dress was slightly raised; her feet rested on the bright fender; and an unread book lay open upon her knees. The door was opened quietly.

"A lady wishes to see you, miss. She will not give her name."

"Never mind, let her come in, Bertha. No, you need not light the lamp."

She did not change her position till her visitor entered.

When the door again opened, she rose, pushed away the chair, and turned. Before her was a lady—tall, in deep mourning, and with a veil on, which its wearer did not offer to raise.

"I have come to you as a suppliant—upon the subject of—my—my son."

"Yes?"

"You surely will not marry him?"

"Not marry him? Surely I shall."

"No, no! I beg—I beseech—I implore of you to have mercy on—on me—his mother— on him—on us all. You do not love him—you cannot love him—you cannot."

"That I *cannot* love him, as you mean it, I might question; but I will not deny that I *do not* love him. That is no reason why I should not marry him. He knows I do not love him; but he thinks—and perhaps he thinks rightly— that I shall be to him as good a wife—yes, as good a wife—as he will find elsewhere."

"Oh! I would give you all—all I possess. What is it you would have? Seven, eight, a thousand a-year ; but you must not marry him. I—I—his mother—I love him—nursed him— taught him to pray—live for him—by him. My husband is gone ; he is my—my great hope, and now, now, you tell me, tell me you will make this sacrifice, and God—yes, God will see to you."

"You forget," answered the girl, with quiet rebuke, "that a mother, though perhaps not in luxury, bore *me*, nursed me, and would have taught me to pray, I doubt not, if—if I had not lost her. The narration of misfortune on mis- fortune would not—Ah, I know it well—would not justify—no, not justify, would not excuse— me in your eyes. You would receive from me a favour, but nothing more ; not even an expla- nation. You are ready to give me money, but never pardon."

" You wrong me, indeed you wrong me: God will pardon, shall not I ? "

" Fine words, fine words. God will do more than pardon. He will call me child ; will you ? Oh, I know your language; *I* read my Bible too. I am bold enough, even now, to call him Father;

and you—you come, not to beg me not to call you mother, but not to make you such in your own despite. Yes, God pardons; I did not need you to tell me, in order to be sure of that."

"But to marry whom you own you do not love, will He pardon *that?*"

"I cannot say; but if He will not, your drawing-rooms, madam, let me tell you, are often crammed with the forms of the Unforgiven! Perhaps you know more of God than I know, and are right in telling me of his ways; but I, girl as I am, know more of men than—yes, thank your God for it—than you will ever know. Perhaps I cannot give love; you say I cannot; I am not asked for it. There is one thing I shall give, whether asked or not, a thing usually promised though the promise be not always kept,—fidelity. Pardon me, there are not many women who would love your son; I at least (though you may be unable to understand this) respect him, in my way. He says —perhaps, again, you fail to comprehend— that he cannot be happy without me; I will strive to make him happy with me. It is not an affair of yesterday ; it is I who have resisted and waited for conviction. He has convinced me ; and neither a mother's love nor a woman's scorn will change me. Try to change him, and I will not oppose you. You will never acknowledge me as your daughter ; you must see that you only insult the painful position from which I am going to escape, if you are not sufficiently successful to keep me in it."

"Heaven knows I would not keep you in it. I would save you from it, will save you from it. But why do you ask such a sacrifice?—the sacrifice of my son ? I tell you I will give you—"

"Enough, enough. You are proud that you have been a wife, madam ; I will be one, too, even your son's. You have exhausted your arguments, and all but my self-command. I would rather you went." And she rang her bell hastily.

"Who is that—who is that I met on the staircase ?" asked Reginald, eagerly, as he burst into the room. "Who was it, Lettice, who was it ? "

"Never mind who it was ; I am not at liberty to say."

"Very well, very well ; I don't care ; am sorry I asked. See : I came to ask you to help me—to help me as you have helped me before. That old screw of a grandfather has sent me no money, and I want to go into the country for a couple of days. Really, I am ashamed to ask you, Lettice, but you are always so—"

" How much do you want ? "

" Oh ! a big sum, rather, if I can get it. Ten pounds."

"I can give you seven, but no more." She put out her arm to keep him back. " No, Reginald, there is my hand; it is enough—you must not kiss me."

" Why not ? "

" Sit down. I want to tell you something."

But as she spoke, there came another knock, and again Bertha entered.

" Please, miss, Mr. Cyril Vavasour wishes to see you particularly, he says."

" The devil he does ! " exclaimed Reginald. " I don't wish to see him—at least here.

Where shall I go, Lettice? See, I can go into the inner room, and then on to the staircase, and so out, whilst he is with you here. Thanks for the money. All right. Don't say I was here."

"Go, go. Tell Mr. Vavasour to come upstairs, Bertha."

She went and looked at herself inquisitively in the glass, turning from it as the door was re-opened and admitted Vavasour. He came forward unhesitatingly, and offered his hand.

"You were right, you see, in your prophecy. I *have* come first to ask a favour ; and this time I think you will grant it, though again it refers to Reginald Dormer."

"And it is——"

"Why, the young fool has left London ; has, in fact, eloped with a girl whom I know."

"How long since ? "

He looked at his watch.

"Just three hours ago. The girl does not, cannot care for him, or I would not raise my finger in the matter. She is using him for one of her purposes. I am in a position to let him know the truth. When he knows it, let him please himself. They are making for the border, and for Thistlewood." ·

" Thistlewood ! "

" Yes. Now you understand, perhaps, why I come to you. I remembered at once your telling me that you were born there, and know the country by heart. One blunder in the pursuit might be fatal to my overtaking them in time to prevent the mischief contemplated. You will come ? "

" Yes, I will accompany you with pleasure. But how do you come by all this information ? "

" Through the girl's maid." Lettice turned to the fire and poked it.

" Yes—well ? "

" No sooner has this woman helped in the scheme, and they have started, than, left alone, she repents, and comes to me with the story. Could I not prevent the marriage, and yet keep the adventure a secret ? Like all repentant people, she seemed more in an agony than in her senses."

Again Lettice poked the fire.

"Thistlewood is close to his grandfather's place—to Mr. Chesterfield's," he continued. "Did he ever tell you that?"

"Oh, yes! And I know Thistlewood Manor as well as Rotten Row. But when are we to start?"

Again he looked at his watch.

"In an hour and a half. Can you be ready?"

"I am ready now."

"It's a fatiguing journey. We shall spend all the night in the train; and we shall have to post the whole of to-morrow. Be ready by six, and I will call for you."

"Good! You may depend on me."

CHAPTER XII.

THISTLEWOOD is on the border-land, the scene in former centuries of many a splendid harry, the shelter of many a titled robber. The hills that rise in lines all but parallel along its limits are of considerable range, though not of height. But their bleak and barren sides had once won for them a border proverb. It had seemed as if in those brackeny wastes Nature bore tenderer offspring only, like the mothers of Lacedæmon, to expose them to die, scorning to suckle any save the sturdy scions impregnated by the spirit of the storm. But Time and the temper of man have somewhat broken that sullen chain of mountains, and made outlying plots at least subserve the necessities of the altered days. Aided by fire and the harsh strokes of the harrow, cultivation has stealthily

climbed those heights, long deemed inaccessible ;
barley waves its beneficent banner on slopes
where once the heather would scarcely bloom ;
and partridge-broods stir the autumn corn where
the bittern boomed over the morass, and the
blackcock called along the crags. Yet ever
and anon Nature seems to stir, and claim from
the theft of man her appanage and her home.
Fierce storms awake in the cradle of the hills,
and shriek aloud for the parent they have lost.

"Great Heavens ! what a night ! Can you
shelter here ? "

" Anywhere, if *you* can. I know these nights
of old ; have been out in them on those horrible
hills hundreds of times. What a pity the place
is in ruins ! The outhouses are best, and the
horses will not take much harm ; so I don't see
that it matters much."

There was no grate, but there was a fire-
place, and a chimney with a draught that had
not been fed for months ; it sucked up the
smoke and heat from the huge logs, that she
had already gathered and set a-blazing, with a
hungry roar.

"I have not forgotten how to make a fire," she said, as Vavasour returned from the stable; "Come and dry yourself; you are nearly wet through in helping the man with the carriage; he could have done it himself. Oh, it is not so bad, after all; the windows are more or less right. What a glorious fire! No, take that yourself, whatever it may be; I can sit on these logs."

It had been a comfortable cottage once, and, fortunately for them, had consisted of a second story. The roof was broken in in parts; the rain pattered on the rafters overhead, and even began in places to drip through upon them. Still, the door closed, in a fashion; only a couple of panes were broken; and the fire glowed like a cyclopean furnace. And there they sat by it; the boy who left his home; the girl who was kind to him in his self-imposed but difficult exile, with the separation and the experience of the years to meddle with the sensations of their meeting—Cyril, and Tiny Forde. Yet were they again together; the boy burst into the man, the girl grown into the woman. Her large handsome cloak was gathered round her, and over the large unshapen logs; her hair, travel-loosened, hung waywardly down; her delicate hands, free from jewels, were simply clasped upon her knee; her large, unwandering. eyes, that had lost no lustre, centred upon him; and her look and figure, from the spot where she sat, fawned as of old, though with none of the old tenderness, upon the once warm friend, now callous stranger, who addressed her. Through every change she had preserved this pristine peculiarity which had won him long ago!

During the journey they had exchanged but few sentences. He had attended to her wants, and for the rest had preserved a guarded cold- ness, which she had met with a cheerful interest in everything on the route, except himself. It is not difficult to be silent in a railway-carriage, nor even (if you particularly desire it) in a post-chaise; and so their conversation had all along been meagre. They would have to talk now, if they intended to stay where they were for any length of time.

"Very odd, *very* odd," he said, "that we
should hear nothing of them anywhere! I fear
we shall miss them. What an idiot the boy is!
and that—that—" he was not audible—"of a
girl!"

"There is no fear of our missing them," she
answered, with marked quietness; they *must*
enter Thistlewood by this road, that's certain,
and pass through Flinton, that last village, you
know. No, we shall not miss them."

He felt annoyed that her manner should be
such a contrast to his own; that she should
speak with a calm confidence, and he with a
hesitating anxiety. He was silent again.

"Do you remember Emma?" she asked, after
a long pause.

He started.

"It was Emma; of course, it was Emma."

"What—who was Emma?"

"Whom I saw the other night."

"Where?"

"On a door-step in the Strand—dead."

"Dead! Dear, dear! I got an almost un-
readable letter from her a week ago, begging

for assistance. I was at Brighton when it arrived, and so it lay in London a fortnight. I drove to the address it gave—some dreadful slum in Drury Lane—as soon as ever I read it, but she was not there, and no one could help me. Dead! on a doorstep! Cold and hunger, I suppose; and I might have saved her had I known sooner. The evenings we have spent together!"

"We? Yes, both of us. I remember well."

"Ah! and so do I. How I loathed her after the night you suddenly left! We never spoke again, though we met often."

"Loathed her! Why did you loathe her?"

She stared steadily at him.

"The time for affectation has, I should think, left you; yet the time that has come might have enlightened you without appealing to me. If you did not know then, you might have looked back since with the eyes of your experience, and guessed why I loathed her. I loathed her because she taught you to loathe me—to loathe and leave me. I know well enough what hurried you home; you shrank from the hand that had never done anything but nursed you. Nay, I am not taunting; the idea of taunting a man for what he did eight years ago! Of course you are wiser now, and shrink as little from this journey with me as I shrink from telling you of a love which I no longer feel. She is dead!—hah!—on a door-step; you are—aye, I know it—like your neighbours; and I—I am going to be married. You were right to go, after all; though you left me a gold heart, which I have yet, and a living, sorrowing heart, which I have got rid of. I kept even the last a long time, though. I was in earnest when I asked you to stoop to be my friend. I think your refusal completed my emancipation."

"I had no option but to refuse, as I thought and felt then; a year later I should have granted your request."

"A year later I should not have made it," she replied; "but tell me, if you will—I am curious—a year later would you have made *your* request?"

" About Reginald?"

" Yes, about Reginald. Would you ? "

" Yes. Were there any use in it, I would renew it now. That I am here is some proof."

" True ; we remain interested in people from habit, long after the motive has left us. That *I* am here is a proof of *that.*"

" I have answered you one question ; will *you* answer another ? Since you say, or insinuate, that you are here from your former interest in me, why did you refuse *my* request when you were sufficiently interested to implore my friendship ? "

" Oh yes, I will answer it ; it has ceased to be of importance. Reginald Dormer has a sister, or had. A sister is naturally interested in her brother ; you owned to a similar interest in the boy ; *my* interest at once extended to all the three. The explanation is simple. I said that you should come back, and I intended that you should. I came to give up both the desire and the intention ; but you see you have come, for all that. Fate survives our poor plots ; and, as I say, I am going to be married—to a friend of yours—while Emma freezes to death on a doorstep."

"A friend of mind. May I ask his name?"

"Frank Morley only. His mother had not left me ten minutes when you called yesterday; had but just risen from her knees— yes, her knees—imploring me not to marry her son."

He made her almost start from her seat by the loud gust of laughter with which he leaped from his, and momentarily drowned the howl of the night wind. He strode up and down the rain-dabbled floor, with his arms outstretched and his head flung back, breaking out again anon into short, sharp laughs of harsh pleasure that were anything but pleasant to hear. He was telling to himself again the gossip that had grated on him so when he heard it from the lips of the flaxen-haired doll in the London ball-room, the fairest flower from whose bouquet he had won with tender looks and tender words, and then cursed and crushed beneath his heel.

"Ha, ha! there *are* distinctions, you know,"

he said aloud, repeating the words that he had never forgotten ; "there *is* a difference between them. What would they all give to annihilate it now ? "

She had quite recovered from the effect of his first wild outbreak, and sat composedly gazing at the fire. It did not seem his pleasure to enlighten her as to his soliloquy, so she would not notice it.

" Have you ever published your poem ! " she asked at length, when, though still walking about the room, his face had settled into a smile.

He stopped, as if recalled to her presence.

" Um—er—pardon me. My poem ? Oh no ; am just where I was, Tiny, eight years ago, or further back, since *you* believed in me then, and no one believes in me now. So you are going to marry Morley ? " He resumed his seat. " And Mrs. Morley wants to dissuade you, and cannot ? "

" And cannot. The morality of moral people strikes me as singular. She is pious, at any rate, and comes and offers me money not to get married. Truly, money is sufficiently abundant, without her generosity; and the love of virtue more plentiful than she seems to fancy, even in places where she imagines there is none at all. But in those places, as well as in others with which she is better acquainted, the virtue which is its own reward is not over safe. The virtue that wins a husband and an income is the virtue that can best be relied on; I find morality ready made for me, and I am going to accept it."

He knew well enough how his own mind had grown in the eight years, but he looked, and marvelled if it had developed as extensively as her own. Yet, was there any cause for wonder, except the wonder of conceit? The capacity for development is limited neither to sex nor sphere, and the circumstances that encourage the capacity had been at least as favourable to her as to him.

"Yes, yes;" he said, musingly. "Security and certainty are the aims of our constant endeavours, and you are right to prefer the harbour of a home."

"You think so now, do you? Yet you left yours for an object which you own you have not even yet at all accomplished—nay, which perhaps you have abandoned. I may have left mine for a reason less paltry than yours, but with a result more disastrous. Suppose I grant that the gratification of self was the motive of both (it certainly was yours), you may talk of your whim where you like, and, at most, people will laugh. Talk of mine, and many will refuse to talk to you at all. See, I have driven the cattle home from those hills on nights to which this is gentle ; half clothed, ill-fed, never thanked ; I have scrubbed that floor."

" This ! "

" Yes, this. This cottage where we sit was my home for years. Do you ask me if I deplore my change ? I should lie if I told you I did. I would rather recline by a fire than make it ; I would as lief be petted by a lord as sworn at by a boor. It is pleasanter—have you tried it ?—to loll in a carriage than to shuffle barefooted and bleeding along the flinty, miry lanes." She drew her tresses forward, and played with them against her cheek. "Perfumes in the hair are preferable to snow and sleet; and there is a magic in the notes of operatic music which you would fail to find in the lowing of cattle heard in the pauses of the winter wind. Virtue its own reward! No, the world is arranged differently to that. It is a doctrine not difficult to preach when one hand reposes on a velvet cushion, and the other grasps a lace handkerchief worked by the prettiest lambs of a pet fold. I like this lama cloak; it is warmer and softer than serge, or none at all. Which would Mrs. Morley prefer, or her daughters, think you? I fancy we should be found to agree. I do not like this damp stone floor, do you?" She shivered. "It does not suit my thin boots, or my constitution. Who has arranged it for me that I am not scrubbing it still, or dead, like Emma, upon another?"

"You are not defending yourself to me, surely? It is altogether unnecessary."

"I am defending myself, perhaps, against myself; but I am going to marry Morley, and

shall have no one then to defend myself against
—except his mother."

"Defend yourself against whom you will,
you solve no riddles for me.   We each of us
think our own history the great practical paradox ; I have my history too.   It is something
for us to be sitting here, and both pretty well
satisfied ; we are neither of us without a clue
to the great enigma."

It was spoken aloud, and yet scarcely to her.
Immediately he added, rising :

" It seems to me we shall be here all night ;
it is well we are supplied with provisions ; I will
have some, you had better do the same."   He
opened the door and called out to the post-boy
who was in the stable.

" He says he is sure nothing has passed.   It
rains and blows harder than ever, and there is
snow too, now.   We had better warm the wine ;
you will do it better than I."

" There is a risk of cracking this bowl, but I
will try."   She bent over the fire.

" Really, I don't understand this, they *must*
be ahead of us."

"No, they are not ; I have good reason for knowing."

" What do you know ? "

"I know," she answered, stirring the wine with a broken twig, " that your friend, whoever she may be, did not leave London yesterday with Reginald Dormer at the time you fancy."

" How can you possibly know that ? "

" Because I saw Reginald three hours after you suppose he started. He left my room yesterday, just as you entered it."

" As I entered it ! And he did not leave London by the same train as we did, most certainly ; therefore we must have left him ——"

" In town. Exactly."

" And you knew this all along ? "

" How could I help knowing it ? "

" D—n ! And you——"

To find oneself a fool by the machinations of others, is the most unpleasant discovery that a man can make. Horribly it dawned upon him that he had been made such by three people, one, if not two of whom had the greatest possible motive to make him ridiculous, whilst the third could enjoy a joke like the rest of the world. The idea of a man being such an ass as to believe the mere word of a waiting-maid. His companion still attended to the sherry.

"And you are in the plot with Miss"—he checked himself—"with them to carry out this silly scheme ? "

"With whom ? Nay, I am no one's confidante, not even yours, and certainly not Reginald's. He simply called to ask me for what he has often asked before—money ; and when you came with your story, I became a little curious to see how my money was to be applied. Besides, I fancied the journey ; it has already amused me. I think they will come ; yes, yes, they will come ; though I know as much as I have told you, not a word more. The sherry is quite ready, but we have no sugar."

He stood and thought.

"Very well. This much is clear. Either— though you are not in it—they have played a poor joke, or she wished me to know of the meditated elopement and go after her ; or rather, to start before her and prevent it. In either case my part in the affair is over. I am going to return, if you are not."

He opened the door. Distinctly came the sound of wheels and hoofs : the pace was a gallop. She hastily joined him at the threshold. The vehicle, though invisible, was audibly close upon them. Above the stamp of the horse's feet, and the rattle of the wheels, shot up a voice into the night. " For Heaven's sake ! Oh ! there ! Yes—great——"

A stumble, a fall, a splashing sound, followed by a shower of wet and mud, and the silence was complete.

Vavasour rushed into the hut, snatched a log that was well a-flame from the hearth, and hurried back. Before him was a horse that had shaken itself from the broken shafts. Blanche Latimer, her teeth set, her right hand grasping her left wrist, her face pale as the falling flakes ; and Tiny on her knees in the road, supporting with her arm the head of Reginald Dormer.

" Yes, yes—so ; he is not too heavy for you ? Slowly—slowly ; let the weight fall on me. Mind the door ! Down now, down."

They laid him before the fire, placing his back against the logs. Snow was in his golden hair, snow on his smooth face, snow on his dabbled breast ; but side by side with the snow, on his hair, on his lips, on his vest, was blood! his own.

"It's no use—it's no use ; he's dead—stone dead ! "

" Dead ! No, no, not dead! " And the figure, which had stood huddled against the door, rushed to the motionless corpse.

" Yes, dead ! and *you* have killed him. Leave him, both ! You pair of Sybarites ! leading him with your wily wantonness to his death. You liked his smooth cheeks—look at them now. Off ! I say. Reginald ! Reginald ! I was to be kind to you, for her sake ; and I shall bring her—your corpse."

The postilion stood by, amazed and helpless.

"Don't stand there, dolt ! The horses, put them to at once. *You* come, either of you ! Where are you to go ? What is it to me ? Comfort each other, as you are well able."

"I am ready, sir."

" Then, to Mr. Chesterfield's. Here, help me, boy! You know the manor ? "

They placed the heavy inanimate body as best they could inside the carriage, Vavasour following.

" No one comes with me ; no one, I say."

" You *must* return for us; indeed, you must."

" Yes, Miss ; but it'll be a good hour first: it's four good miles each way."

" Now, on! on! as fast as you can." He looked at his watch. " They will yet be up ; but the faster the better. On ! on ! "

CHAPTER XIII

REEKING with sweat, and the wet mud en-
crusting their panting bellies, the post-horses
stood before the iron gates of Thistlewood
Manor. The rain and snow had been blown
away : the moon had broken out high up in the
sky, and the tattered clouds scudded across her
pale scared form in mad succession.

"No one at the lodge, sir."

"But you can open the gates, surely ?   Shall
I get out and help you ? "

"No, sir, no ; it's all right ; that's it."

"Mind you go round to the back, and as
quietly as possible."

"Am I to go back for the—the ladies,
sir ? "

"Yes, if you like.   You will find me to-
morrow at the Swan in Thistlewood. I suppose

T

you will stay there to-night; you don't intend posting back home till the morning ? "

" Hardly, sir. Them horses is all but done. But where will the ladies want taking to ? "

"I can't tell you. I don't know. That is their affair. But,—look you,—have the sense to hold your tongue about this accident. The family may not want an inquest, or any-thing about it to get into the papers : it will be worth your while to show your discretion."

" I understand all that hard enough. Shall I go on, sir, now ? "

" Yes, quietly." He looked at his watch. " Only half-past ten. Good God! what will she say ? what will she do ? However, I must perform my part as best I can."

He walked round to the front door, where a servant who had assisted in carrying the dead boy into the house promised to meet him. Sin-gularly enough, the door was open ; but he waited till the man arrived.

" Dreadful business this, sir ; better not tell master to-night. He is up and in the library, but probably asleep, and doesn't let any one go near him unless he rings. Better wait till to-morrow."

" Yes, yes ; perhaps we had. But I want to see Miss Dormer."

" You know her, sir ? "

" I know her well. Give her my name— Vavasour—Mr. Vavasour. I will break it to her."

" Very sorry there's no fire, sir, in this room ; but perhaps you would not mind."

" Not at all. Only tell her at once."

He was alone. Could the remembrance of the last time he had sought her fail to rush upon his mind ? Neither then nor now had time been given him to collect his words or his resolution ; each time had circumstance hurried him to her presence, now even more rapidly than then. With the opportunity of hesitation, then and now would he probably have shrunk from his errand. That was not happy even in its commencement : deplorably disastrous in its results. How had this begun ? how would it end ? She was coming : she was before him. He had determined to speak straight away; but her appearance silenced him. How altered even from her former self! Her face, when he had seen it in London, had shown a ruddy health compared to its present pallor; hers seemed a delicacy of life borrowed from death. Yet it was the countenance of Mary Dormer still, and the sight of it jerked into his a hue that had not been in it for months and months, and an uncertainty into his tones to which they had been long a stranger. Her hand, which she gave him, and which he kept mechanically in his, and she did not offer to withdraw, was cold and unliving.

"I have come, Miss Dormer, with not very good news. Your brother has met with an accident, a severe accident, and there is some ——"

"My brother is dead, is he not? tell me. I see by your face that he is dead. Speak, speak!"

"He is."

He grasped her hand more firmly: he scarce knew what to anticipate; he was ready to accept the worst.

"God's will be done!" she said, simply. The

tears hesitated in her eyes; she closed over them the long dark lashes, as he had so often seen and marked her close them in the golden gone-away days; again she raised them, and the tears seemed to have been sent back. "Thank you, Mr. Vavasour! thank you. I know you were always good to him. You will be good to him just once more—and to me. He must be buried near papa at Onchester—not here—not here; but in the cemetery where papa is—where mamma is. Will you see to it? Of course I shall go to the funeral; and you will—will you not?" Yes, yes—he would do all—all—that she might ask: what more could he do? Nothing; that was all.

And this was the girl whom he had spoken of as the one whose heart six hundred a-year and a mere freak of finance would have brought throbbing—where he had sworn by God's truth that it should never throb—upon his own! He gazed; and he felt that he had foully wronged and foully sworn. Man! you were a boy again, so at this moment you could perfect perjury, and fold her to your form! Fool! you are not

going to torment her now? not about to ask
her if with her brother's corpse you may divide
the empire of her heart? I know not what he
might have done; his looks were very wild;
but her low patient voice summoned him back
from the hot pursuit of his careering brain.

"Do you not hear voices across the hall?
There is somebody with grandpapa; listen!"

She opened the door: through one immediately facing it came the sound, momentarily
growing louder. There seemed to be an altercation. They could catch the words:

"I will know if . . . It's no . . . Now, by
. . . Look you! . . ."

"Oh, Mr. Vavasour! who can it be? They
are both in passion."

Louder grew the voices; louder and more
distinct. They crept into the hall; and clear,
fast, and furious came the words.

"Then, by the God who made us both! I
will know or will strangle you where you
stand!"

They hastened into the room. The old man
held a stout stick high in the air—it was de-

scending; an arm clutched at it, wrung it from his grasp, and flung it on the floor with a laugh of disdain.

The back of the man was turned towards them; the arm might be anybody's; but the scornful laugh was—Vavasour knew it as quickly as he heard—the laugh of Guy Blacklock.

"Curse it! shut the door!" foamed out Mr. Chesterfield. "Would you have my menials see this fellow? . . . Well, then—the woman is rotting in Thistlewood churchyard, and be d——to her! as you would have been long ago, if curses could kill."

"I might have wronged him, not he me!" exclaimed Blacklock, bitterly. And pulling his hat over his eyes, and without a glance of recognition at Vavasour, he hurried from the house. The old man had sunk back into his chair.

"Come away; come away!" Mary whispered, and drew Vavasour from the room. "I know not what this is; but it is terrible! terrible! but I shall leave it all now. Go, Mr. Vavasour! please, go! I will come to Onchester with poor Reginald; you will be there? Thursday will be the best day, if it will suit you."

" And the hour ? "

" Half-past ten."

" And you can do the rest yourself, here ? "

"Quite well—quite well. Go, go! He has rung his bell, and may want me ; thank you ! thank you ! Heaven reward you, I cannot." He walked round to the back of the house again, took one last look at Reginald, kissed the callous lids he had never kissed before, and turned away. Down the long winding avenue he slowly strode, defiant of the bitter wind, and would-be defiant of the bitterer sorrow. Faster and faster scampered the loosened clouds; more and more scared looked the distracted moon, as though she would retire into herself, or away from their unkind mockery, and could not. He approached the iron gateway. Over a wicker paling by its side, but without, leaned a figure gazing into the grounds. Vavasour stood and fronted him ; he started.

" Vavasour ! "

" Yes ; did you not see me just now ? "

" See you! Where ? "

" There ; in the manor ; with your—your—your father."

" No, no ; wait." He threw back his hair. " Let me think. Surely—yes—some one came into the room whilst I was with—with him " (he seemed to avoid the name that Vavasour had used). " Was it you ? "

" I was one. A girl whom I have known long, and whom I must conclude to be your niece, was the other."

Quite disregarding the question, he exclaimed, quickly and fiercely :

" What did you hear ? "

" The first I heard," said Vavasour, quietly and slowly, " was a threat sufficiently horrible ; but it was from *you.*"

" Oh, he had maddened me ! You did not hear, then, what preceded it ; if you had ! Oh, if you had ! I besought him with lip service, with the accents of a beggar, with the humility of a galley-slave ; and for what ? Simply to tell me if Nelly lived ; or, if she was dead, where she lay — or anything, anything that could assure me of her fate, even if it was the worst. He mistook my mood; at first, he used me with a stupid silence, then with taunts, at last with jeers and ridicule; and in my wild passion I told him I would wring from him either what he knew, or his life's breath. It was then you entered. Did you see the paltry rage with which he struck at me? His impotence recalled me to myself. You heard his final words; they drove me from his presence, for I feared to stay, lest at last I might fulfil my threat. Good God!"

He relapsed into silence, leaning over the gateway, and gazing into an invisible land. The strange fact, altogether unaccounted for, that Vavasour should be at Thistlewood Manor —the new light which had of necessity dawned upon him as to Blacklock's real name and birth— the singularity of their meeting, so shortly after the assurance that they would meet no more,— these would have suggested to most people, if not curious questioning, at least a passing remark. But Blacklock neither inquired, nor appeared to wonder. And as for Vavasour, had he too not reason to find in silence companionship enough ? Who was this strong, outlawed man, whose words had awakened him to new worlds of thought ; whose history, so recently told, had been banished from his mind only by occurrences whose relationship to self had made for a time more predominant ? The brother of that May Chesterfield, whose daughter had been—aye, still was, the magnet of his life! The old evenings at Onchester came back before him ; scene chasing scene rushed across his mind ; but ever mingling with the brightest, the two orphans, the dead brother, the living sister, the grave of the Artist and poor May. Death over some—Sorrow over all. Love and Hate, Genius and Failure, contradictions and contrasts inextricably intertwined.

" A melancholy errand," Vavasour said at last, " brought me to Thistlewood ; it is my first visit. I never saw Mr. Chesterfield but once before ; but Mr. Dormer I knew well. Your sister I never knew. That was their orphan who was with me. Did you see her ? "

" No."

"I brought her the news of her brother's death, your sister's other child ; your nephew, in fact."

"I suppose so," he said ; "I suppose so. Both Dormer's children. I recollect meeting him in Italy, his runaway marriage with May, and that man's curses, and his forbidding the whole family to correspond with them in any way. That was six months before—before my—you know what I would say. It is idle for me to pretend that I care for, or am interested in, the death of the boy, or the life of the girl of whom you speak ; that I care for any of them. Oh, Nelly ! Nelly ! you thought you had none of my love, and you had it—all !"

"Come," said his companion, "come away. It is perhaps but poor consolation to offer, but there may be truth in the words he spoke, for they were spoken in passion. She *may be* lying asleep in Thistlewood churchyard, and there, perhaps, you may discover memorials to reconcile you at once to the past and the future."

Blacklock stopped suddenly and faced him.

" There is something in what you say—something in what you say. Thanks! thanks! Oh, yes! yes! something in what you say." They walked on.

Varasour himself was forced internally to own that he at least could not see anything in his own suggestion. What could bring Nelly to Thistle-wood at all? Why should she be buried there? Fearful to encourage a false hope, he at length hinted his doubts.

"No! you were right at first," Blacklock answered, doggedly. "Strange that I should not have thought of it before! It is certain—certain—that his inducing me to remain at Thistlewood those few weeks before returning to the University was part of a scheme; certain that by some devilish machination he misled both mother and daughter, and removed them beyond the power of my discovery; certain that he knew where they were when I rushed back home and taxed him with deceiving me. What more likely than that he should eventually bring Nelly within his immediate power — here — here; and that, after I know not what cruel sorrows, she died, and lies where the savage said she was rotting. Would to God she died —died soon! "O yes, yes! it *would be* a consolation to know that she slept there or anywhere, either with grass or waves, or what you will, above her. I should be reconciled; I should be reconciled. But not to know—to know nothing; to be in agonising ignorance whether she wastes her days in a cellar, a hospital, a prison; to be blind to all, and so be forced to dwell upon the worst; it is horrible: so horrible, that it drove me again with submission to seek that relentless man whom I must own as father. There may be truth in his words. God grant I may find it so! I ask for nothing better than to know—know beyond question that she is dead."

"Do you mind — walking — more — more slowly?" asked Vavasour; "you blow me." His companion's strides were immense, and every moment increased. "How far are we from Thistlewood village?"

"Not more than a mile now."

"Well, I sleep there to-night—at the Swan; there is such an inn, is there not?"

" There used to be."

" Well, sleep there, too ; to-morrow we can talk this over, and perhaps discover the truth ; at least the mere truth with which you say you will rest satisfied."

" Be it so ! "

They walked on in silence till they reached the village ; it was past midnight, and they had to rouse the landlord of the Swan from sleep.

" Any room for us ? "

" Plenty, sir—plenty."

There was no talk of supper that night ; silently they separated to their respective chambers ; but Vavasour had only just begun to undress, when a knock was given at his door, followed by the entrance of Blacklock.

" I *must* come to you again. Do you really think I may hope ? do you think we shall find her grave ? Oh, if the day would dawn ! "

He strode up and down the room. Vavasour sat upon the bed. Was this, he thought, the sneering, defiant, haughty man, whose words of reckless challenge to the world's opinions and the heart's affections had so often made uneasy

his blood ?   Excited, nervous, pitifully anxious,
he came to ask a question anew which a child
would scarcely have put once, and no one could
answer him.   "Do you think there is hope ?   I
have wandered up and down country ways, and
foul town alleys, peering into rose-guarded cot-
tages and fever-held cellars, ever on the gaze
for Nelly's face.   I kept that toll-bar, thinking
she might some day pass.   I have given up the
search again and again, but ever to return to it.
The thought of her has whipped me into re-
newals of my melancholy journeys.   She looked
at me from every book I read as soon as I came
to love it ; she peeped at me through the
blossoming spring hedges ; she gazed at me
from the surface of the snow, ever with one face
—the face of her as I saw her last.   Can we
not summon up the sun ?   Vavasour, Vavasour !
is there—is there hope ? "

"My dear fellow ! you must speak more calmly,
or no discovery could bring you peace.   With
that face of which you speak you can never
hope to see her.   If she is dead—yes, dead—
and you come to know it, you must believe (and

it is probable) that she died without too much
suffering, and with some kind thoughts of you.
Sit here, and listen to me. After all, would
it not be better to believe without further in-
quiry? He said she was dead : doubtless she
is ; and if she be in that quiet churchyard,
there's an end."

"No, no! there is not an end. When I left
her, I left her, I am sure, with the capacities of
a mother! Even if she be dead, and dead
down there, a son—a daughter—maybe both—
tread, perhaps, this earth where for that sad
possibility I remain a vagrant. I may solve
this doubt, too : is it, unsolved, less fearful than
the other? Oh! in this life of mine, in which
Action has been forbidden me, Thought has
thriven with pestilent and unrestful growth;
and Thought has shown to me that generation
is the only act—and it the most responsible
and irreparable of all—which man can altogether
control. It accomplished, he can do little
more than accept consequences, be they what
they may. My religion—my beliefs—are not
the acknowledged beliefs of my kind ; but I

have them : and I swear to you, by the God of all, that I have never exercised that power since I last lay by Nelly's side ! "

There was silence, save in the palpitation of that vast and agitated form.

"But you yourself," said Vavasour at length, " confess that the consequences are not in our own hands ; clearly, the consequences of your act are beyond the power of yours. But I will suppose that she is dead ; and, further (though the supposition is arbitrary), that a child of hers —and of yours—survives. Son or daughter, his or her age would be, as I understand from what you told me the other night, about my age —twenty-five. Suppose a son ; suppose him found. I do not wish to harrow, but I wish to persuade. He may be—we are on suppositions, and such things have happened—a proud young patrician, who would not know you ; or a con- demned felon, whom you would not know." Blacklock shook his head sceptically. "Sup- pose a daughter, and her found. Again we are on suppositions. She may be the wife of a man brought up in the rigid orthodoxy of social creeds, and the discovery of what the world calls her illegitimacy might be as unwelcome to her as to him; or she may be an illiterate menial—nay, a polluted outcast, whether in splendour or in rags."

"O Vavasour! Vavasour! You are young, but I thought your insight was truer than this. I will not upbraid you; for God has gifted you, and you will live to see differently. But do you talk to *me* of felons and of outcasts? You may think yourself superior to both. I do not presume to exalt myself above either. And if these were my offspring—felon or outcast—I made them what they are. Look you, Vavasour!"—he placed his hand firmly upon the young man's shoulder—"to find an idiot would be hard; to find an intellect only raised above an idiot's by its reasoning depravity would be little less so; to find a felon would scarcely bring much comfort to the eyes of a father; to find—for I understand you, and you are right to put your case forcibly when all are suppositions—to find a harlot would, you think, be a discovery better left alone. But I say to you,

I would be nurse to my idiot, I would fondle my felon, protect, as parent and priest, my penitent prostitute, so I found in the cell or the gutter Nelly's child and mine! Are we immortal, or are we not? Have we souls, or bodies only? If, as some believe, we have individual souls, with the privilege of immortality—souls whom sin can stain, but whose stains One Great Father can cancel, shall the accidental father, with the stains on his own, shrink from the stains that assoil his child's? If but material bodies, with gift of transitory life, why, sin is like any other stain that simple skill can remove. And do I refuse your hand because, an hour ago, it was splashed with mud? We prate of piety and pardon; but we are too proud to touch any sores except our own, and then only to hide them. You argue ill; or, if you argue well, you argue idly. I have, perhaps, a clue to the labyrinth of my life; I will follow it, if it be to the steps of the gibbet or the threshold of a brothel. Yet do I pray that it will lead me only to the flowers upon Nelly's grave."

"Well, be it so; and I will give what help I

can. Go; and try to sleep. Really, I must; I am worn out with the hardest day I ever had."

Vavasour, however, did not sleep soundly; and woke very easily to the knock of the boots, announcing eight o'clock.

"There's a young lady below wants to see you, sir," he said, when he brought hot water; "as soon as you are dressed, if you please, sir."

He was sorry he had let the man go without asking her name. He would ring. No; what did it matter? It could be but either Miss Dormer, Blanche Latimer, or Tiny Forde: it might be just as well to go on dressing; he had plenty to occupy his mind, without knowing beforehand what fresh complexity might have arisen. He went down-stairs.

"This is the lady's room, sir!"

He entered. Before a breakfast-table, pouring water from the kettle into the teapot, was Tiny Forde. He had not failed already to reflect that he had last night treated her both with injustice and discourtesy. She had undertaken a long, wearisome journey at his request; and he had left her in the lurch when its difficulties were at their highest; left her, too, with rebukes which, if they were merited, were at least inappropriate. He quite expected to hear no measured accusation of his behaviour; but, to his surprise and ease, she greeted him with perfect calmness and good-humour.

"You were not over-courteous last night," she said; "but I sent for you, not to scold you, but to enlighten you."

"I *was* both rude and unjust, and I am sorry for it; but I was distracted with the sudden passion of grief. It was not your doing, at any rate. Where did you spend the night?"

"Here, to be sure. The chaise returned for us; and you had not arrived when we got here. I inquired for you."

"And—er—— ?"

"Miss Latimer? You see I have learned her name, and a good deal more. She came on with me here, but started back at once in another chaise to Flinton, where she had left her maid—your agonised informant. Really, you have been very blind; but men *are* dull in these matters."

"Perhaps they are ; but I think I see clearly enough now. However, tell your story."

"I never saw any one so unintelligible as she was at first ; I began to think she had gone mad. Beyond spraining her wrist, she had not received any damage from the fall ; but I certainly thought she had lost her wits. I gathered a connected story from her in the end. How, with your knowledge of what had passed between you, you could have been duped by her maid's tale, I cannot understand. Why, it seems the girl has been madly in love with you ; that (of course, as she makes out) you have behaved very badly, and that she wanted to save her pride at Reginald's expense. She had not the slightest intention of marrying him ; but the poor boy was as wild about her as she was about you. She thought you cared for her sufficiently to be jealous of him."

Vavasour laughed aloud.

"She thought so, I say, and so found in him a convenient tool. But you see it all ? "

"Of course I do, though it was a bold stroke. How fatally it has turned out." He was silent a moment. "As you say, I was an idiot to believe that maid. But how came they to be in a gig, such a night as it was, and how did the accident occur? Did she explain that?"

"Why, you see, she was all along anxious for delay, he for haste. He feared to be overtaken, she not to be overtaken. At the stage before Flinton—what's the name of it?"

"I know where you mean."

"Yes. Well, it was here he lost his temper, and threatened to turn back altogether if she would not yield to his scheme of saving time by leaving the maid behind, and going forward in a gig; post-horses they could not get till the following morning. They had not gone a couple of miles from Flinton before he fancied that he heard horses' feet in full pursuit. He drove faster and faster. It became clear to her that he would insist on the marriage being performed as soon as ever they found themselves across the border. And so she would be driven, either by further excuses for delay, to cause him to doubt and then and there desert her (as he had already threatened), or to tell him plainly that she had no intention of marrying him ; and in either case her object, that of mortifying you, and sheltering herself against your indifference, would be lost. The accident solved the puzzle."

" Well, well ; enough of it. She has gone back home, and there's an end. Make breakfast for me too." He rang the bell.

" Where is that gentleman who came with me last night ? "

" He went out very early, sir, and has not yet returned."

" Very well ; that is all I wanted to know. I am going to the churchyard, Tiny, will you excuse me ? "

" Certainly. But might I come with you ? It is ten years since I was there.

" Well, yes ; I don't see why we should not go together. You can show me the way."

They stood among the cradles of the sleeping—the sleeping who have very quiet dreams.

" That is my friend," he said, pointing to

Blacklock, who stood by the porch talking to a
man who was leaning on a clay-dabbled spade.
" No, I don't want to go to him, he is making
some inquiries here."

As he spoke a third man came up to the
porch and admitted Blacklock into the church.
Vavasour went with Tiny vagrant among the
recording tombstones; their inscriptions were
couched in the usual language of bombast and
common-place that makes death even more
ridiculous than life.

" See, this is my mother's."

He read :

" Mary Ellen, wife of Robert Forde."

" She lies alone, I see ; your father lives
then, I suppose ? "

" I suppose so, though I have never seen nor
heard of him since I left Thistlewood, shortly
before I first saw you in London. I fancied we
might possibly find him in that cottage where
we were last night, though I did not wish it, I
confess."

" Not wish to see your father ? "

" I have no desire ; nor is it well to recall

what led me to—to—well, no matter. But I
do not wish to seem in your eyes worse than
I am. Truth is, he was kind neither to me nor
to my mother, and after all that is said about
blood, kindness is the only real relationship.
She was superior to him in every way, and I
think he hated her for it. He was violent ; she
submissive, but melancholy and unloving ; and
I have had to weep often, very often, over
lamentable scenes. I remember so well the
morning they brought her here. It was just
such a morning as this, bright and unclouded
after a night of storm. Had she lived, it had
all been different. I could have helped her to
bear her sorrows, and she—she loved me so
tenderly. And now ! she is there—and I !
See, I always wear this, her last gift, and the
golden heart you left for me, together ; at least
I have done so since poor Reginald carried
away your gift, and you came to restore it.
They are the only two things I possess that,
whatever may have happened since, were given
me from motives that could not be suspected.
So do I prize both. I have been in that large,

pitiless London, houseless, wet, and hungry, but these have never been where"—she paused and smiled—"where your watch once was, Cyril."

He took her hand and fondly pressed it, as though they had been standing by the evening hearth of the little room in Somerset Street.

"It is prettier than my poor golden heart," he said, "but not more gratefully given."

It was an acorn exquisitely worked, and round the rim of the cup were the words, "Your sons shall sit beneath my shade." It and the heart hung side by side; she wore them in her bosom, pendent from a simple black cord, which now, with its kind tokens, hung outside her dress, just as she had drawn them out to show to Vavasour.

"She gave it me when she was dying; hung it round my neck, and died."

"Well?" said Vavasour to Blacklock, who came walking through the wet grass towards them, with a gait that betokened how futile had been his search. "Well?"

"I can make nothing of it, nothing of it. It's no use—no use. There is not a trace, not a clue."

He had just uttered the words when, with a savage hand, and with the speed of the levin, he seemed to aim a blow at Tiny. She screamed, but stood unhurt. The little black cord was snapped in twain, the golden heart was rolling on the grass, and in Blacklock's grasp was the acorn.

Between his fierce fingers he pressed the fragile trinket. There came a sound as of the snap of a clasp, and a paper leaped quickly into the air. As quickly he caught it.

"Vavasour! Vavasour! it is Nelly's hair: Nelly's hair, and mine—mine; just as we twined them when I kissed her last!"

The solemn winter sun was level with the topmost tombs when Vavasour again entered that quiet resting-place, and saw two figures standing by the grave of Mary Ellen Forde. The arm of the strong man had grown into the reliant form of the beautiful girl; and with his unchallenged hand he stroked the hair that had found a worthy home at last upon his stalwart shoulder.

" You know all ? " he asked.

" *All*, Vavasour ! *all !* "

" You have followed your clue, and it has led you—— "

Again he stroked her hair.

" Led me, as I prayed, only to the flowers upon Nelly's grave ! "

※ ※ ※ ※ ※

A few mornings later, and Vavasour was standing by another grave, that yet yawned for its occupant. Sobs and solemn words mingled with the sighs and shudderings of the winter morning ; and the body of the beautiful boy dropped into the indifferent earth. The surviving sister stood more like a mourner summoned by almighty Death from some tomb hard by to do the work of wail, than a real denizen of a quickly-oblivious world. She seemed as though her place was there—by the edge of the grave's chasm—and offered not to stir from the guardianship of the silently-sleeping. All seemed ashamed to trespass on her statue-like regret, till Vavasour took her hand and led her away to the coach that, together with his, had completed the unpretending procession.

" Where were you last night, and where are you going now ? "

" I slept at the Onchester Convent : I am going back to Thistlewood to-day to make some final arrangements, and then I return here. It was only for poor Reginald's sake that I remained in the world ; the motive no longer remains, and next week I rejoin the nuns—to be one of them. I shall always remember your kindness, and shall pray for you. Do as much for me. Good-bye."

The artist's tomb is to be seen by him or her who cares to see it, in quiet Onchester ; and, like those about it, it tells the age (though not like those about it, the merits) of its inhabitant. But close to it is another tomb, on which is simply written :

REGINALD.

CHAPTER XIV.

THE SERPENT'S SEED CRUSHED.

STEPHEN GRAFTON'S room was strewn with saddles, uniforms, sticks, pipes, papers, newly-arrived shirts, boots, belts, gaping portmanteaus ; in fact, everything that betokened departure.

"Welcome, old boy! Come to see the finish? How the deuce my fellow will get all packed in time I can't conceive ; and, personally, I am helpless in the matter. He is off to Bond Street at present about some rascally bridle. Sit down. Pull up to the fire : isn't it cold ?"

He talked as a man talks who *will* be cheerful despite his despondency : a sorry effort ever, and not successful now. Vavasour tried less, and succeeded better ; so that his friend soon fell into the frank display of the regrets he hugged at heart.

"Hang it! old fellow! I know there's no use in my being down, but neither is there any use in pretending to be jolly when one isn't; and *I'm* not, just at present, that's certain. We've never indulged in much demonstration, and that sort of rot; but *you* know if I am sorry to leave you."

"Yes, yes; sorry as I am, Stephen, just, and no more."

"Exactly. But I don't care to hide that I am more cut up about the girl than about leaving you; for you see 'tis more hopeless. I cared for you, old fellow! before I knew her; and I know well enough I shall care for you after I have forgotten her. But, in the meantime, that does not mend matters. She is the only girl I ever really cared for; the only girl I would have left the army for; and now—why, I'd just as soon we went down off Southampton as we didn't. Bah! I'm a fool; but I never talked to you in this way before, and won't again, if we ever meet."

"Meet! Of course we shall meet, some time. You cannot be in Canada more than half-a-dozen years. You shall take a secret with you; I have kept it snug from you long enough; and you will now be the only person to know it—from me at least. This girl you speak of—did it ever strike you that *I* cared for her?"

"Yes, it did; but then you have cared for every nice girl you ever met. I am sure you never once loved one."

"How do one's enemies judge one, if friends see thus? Stephen! Stephen! I loved a girl so well that, loving her, and loving her in vain, has transformed my nature. I believed almost everything; I believe nothing. I would have made shipwreck of my all to save one fellow-being; I would not throw overboard one single thing I value to save the crew of the floating universe. I would have starved in a garret for any object that I thought was worthy; I would not forego a roasted chesnut to achieve the wildest dream that ever philanthrope espoused. I would have gone barefooted and beggared to have gained one honest man's applause; I would as lief have a well-made pair of boots as the cheers of a senate or the benedictions of a country. I cannot speak of Fame without a sneer—fame, which I once held as sacred as Love—the love I bore to her. I am no worse than my neighbours ; but I am more conscious of my worthlessness because I once was different. At first I regretted the change that was not of my seeking ; now I would not change the change even for that love which was sought by us both, and to both denied. True "—he spoke with an unhappy indifference—" self-seeking sometimes grows tiresome ; and virtue and valour, like old flames, are welcomed because we know that they will amuse for an evening without pledging us to-morrow. One is not all forgetfulness ; and I won't deny that, amidst pleasant pastimes—I cannot forego my joke—

> ' medio de fonte leporum
> Surgit a Mary ;

(don't be offended ; perhaps you feel differently to what I do). But even that sentiment is only an intrusion ; and I am well aware that I should soon find love as monotonous as morality or mountains. There, you know it now ; let us say no more about it. I have no desire to

recapitulate my sorrows to my neighbours. I
sometimes go over them to myself when I am
short of something to laugh at. If you have
still any doubts as to my having loved, you
had better question Blanche Latimer. It
was a splendid episode; only she would not
have the sense to regard it as such; she thought,
forsooth, it was to be the very story of life's
drama. But I am growing unintelligible.
Only remember, I pray, that I have loved as
truly and as hopelessly as the best of you. I
can hold up my head with the most scornfully-
rejected of your acquaintance."

"I do not fancy hearing you talk in that
strain," he answered, sadly; "you astonish, but
you still more afflict me. Yet you only show
me that, like myself, you still love Mary Dormer,
but with a love that, unlike mine, you will never
succeed in destroying. You help me to cure
mine, and I am glad of it. Scornful to you I
am sure she never was; scornful to any one she
could never be. God bless her ever for the
kindest words that were ever offered me! I
shall never forget her tender gentleness as she

passed on me the heaviest sentence that mortal could have passed—the sentence of refusal. Had I known what you tell me now, I should never have asked for the heart that you say was denied to you. I am sure I could never gain what you failed to win, and would not have won it if I could. I am glad you have told me; glad you have told me. . . . You know she is in London?"

"No, I do not; I know she is in Onchester— in the convent; she is going to be a nun."

"Oh, you are quite mistaken. She *was* going there; but as soon as Mr. Chesterfield heard of her intention, he raved so that he became at last quite delirious, and the doctors told her plainly that his reason, probably his life, depended upon her remaining with him. They say that he can bear no one near him but her; he is in London, but confined to his bed; I called there a few days ago to say good-bye, and I saw her. She has made up her mind to remain with him whilst he lives, and will go to the Onchester convent afterwards, I suppose. He cannot live very long."

Vavasour stamped.

"For God's sake, Stephen, change the subject ; it is not pleasant to me, and it cannot particularly amuse you. You have said goodbye to your cousin, Lady Harbledown ? "

"I was with Mabel only yesterday evening, and am sorry to leave her too ; she has shown me great kindness." Silence for a time. " Don't you think her very much changed ? "

" Um—yes."

Why this curt monosyllable ?

" Do you see as much of her as you used to do ? "

" Yes."

Still this Spartan brevity.

"I am glad of that. To tell you the truth (I know I can be frank with you, old fellow), I began to fear that some misunderstanding had arisen between you."

"No, none in the world."

" You have not of late spoken of her, nor has she of you, and I thought the silence ominous. I don't know but what I might as well tell you about what perhaps you know already, and if you do not, it may be as well you should, so that you may be on your guard ; that Harbledown has not been to her quite the husband that such a woman deserves."

" May be."

" You remember his giving out that he went abroad because he lost his seat in the House. I believe the fact is that he went to Italy in the trail of one sufficiently notorious, and has returned to England simply because she has. And Mabel, I have no doubt, saw enough in Italy to convince her at last that she was dragged about according to the movements of this very woman. If this be so, and I have pretty good reason to believe it so, she may well be changed."

Vavasour had walked to the window and stood gazing out, but offered no remark to information that, if it was new, ought somewhat to have interested him. His face was turned from that of his friend, and in the latter's might have been seen by a deep observer, during the pause that ensued, an anxious questioning of himself upon some subject strongly entertained, but about which he could not bring himself to break silence. At last, and rather abruptly, he said, pulling out his watch, " Well, Cyril, I yet have one or two good-byes to say, and must needs say them, and so there is nothing else for it but to say good-bye to you."

Vavasour turned round suddenly.

"But I will go with you—at least in your cab."

" No, no ; I would rather you did not."

" But we are to dine together at five, and I shall see you off from the station."

Grafton looked perplexed.

" Indeed no, Cyril ; you see—why—in fact, it's a matter of sentiment, and you must yield to it. I would rather say good-bye to you now, and have done with it."

" If it be a matter of sentiment, it clearly is not one of argument ; therefore be it so."

They would write to each other? Grafton asked. Often. Often, mind ; regularly. Yes, yes ; good-bye, old fellow, said mutually, and there was an end.

There is no pathos like the pathos of silence ;

when we feel that our richest language fails our poorest thoughts, and that it is better to say nothing than to say it wrongly.

"No, no," Vavasour was saying to himself as he walked—whitherwards I scarcely know—"I am wrong to judge him so ; he has nothing to hide from me ; no dearer friend to see, now that I have left him.   The dear old boy is right fond of me, and is glad to get the pain of parting done with.   I grow so suspecting."

I say I do not know, and if I knew I should not perhaps be much wiser myself, or have any information to convey to you, where Vavasour spent the remaining sunlight of that day.   But between seven and eight in the evening he was standing in his chambers, his hat on, and presenting all the appearance of being bent on going out, but as if held back and kept halting by some doubt which he could not resolve.   Yes, he would go.   He extinguished the candle, but the fire still burned brightly, and flung his quiet shadow on the quiet curtains, for again he stood and paused. Should he go ?

"Yes, yes ; enough of these children. I am weary of their pitiful waywardness, of their impatient ignorance. These girls, these dolls! I will annihilate two sorrows, two wrongs, and substantiate one common happiness. More or less, Mabel. Less, or more. Nothing, or all."

Hastily he strode along his passage, hastily tore open his door, and stood upon the staircase. A female figure, dressed in black and veiled, shrank against the wall as he passed. If he noticed her at all with his mind, he doubtless thought that she was on her way to some man's chambers above his ; but dull as might have been his eyes, abstracted as might have been his mind, he turned suddenly at the sound of a voice which he had known in all places, and under all circumstances, as it recalled him with its low but audible murmur :

"Mr. Vavasour."

He re-entered his chambers, she following.

"You once paid me," she said, "what I called a strange visit ; I am paying you, what you will call, a still stranger."

"Strange or otherwise," he answered, "you

are welcome; and I will give you a more patient hearing than you gave to me."

"The expectation of scornful words, even from your lips, would have scarce prevented my coming, when my resolution had conquered obstacles and objections still more severe. I am here where all would say I should not be, no less driven to your presence by my own conscience, than by it I once drove you from mine."

"Conscience is a singular commodity," he said bitterly. "They say that it is given to us to suggest when we are wrong. All I can say is, that the use we make of it is very different. I never find people summon it except to prove to themselves that they are right. We employ it as our hired advocate; I laugh when I hear that its functions are those of a judge. Whom does it ever accuse? Only our neighbours, never ourselves. When a person, man or woman, speaks of conscience, I know he speaks from a foregone conclusion."

"Perhaps," she gently murmured, "I can justify my conduct more successfully to you

than I shall ever be able to justify it to myself.
And yet Heaven——"

She sighed and was silent.

"What would you justify? You were going
to appeal to Heaven. Perhaps *I* am not within
its jurisdiction; still I will say, since it may
impress you, that Heaven knows (and if it does
not, *I* know), that you need no justification for
not—not—(yes, plain words are best), for not
loving me. My self-love will hardly receive
much balm from a visit intended to solve a
riddle which has, in its very question, quite inde-
pendently of the answer, not the most pleasant
of rebukes. Why did you not love me? Really,
I would rather not hear."

"I pray you," she said imploringly, "to listen
rather than accuse. You cannot in your heart
suppose that I come upon any such errand.
You say plain words are best; perhaps they
are, especially when they are parting ones.
And this I know, and this I will say, however
much I lay myself open to the charge of
egotism, that I have had an influence on your
career; aye, am influencing it now. Do I owe

you nothing? Twice have you told me that you loved me; once I believed; will you pardon me? once I doubted. Perhaps I was wrong. But oh, why will men—nay, I will leave the mass, and appeal directly to you—why will you, because some poor girl fastens on your fancy in her own despite, and cannot (or will not, for some reason that she hides) give back the passion that you bestow on her—why, why will you lay at her door and cast upon her conscience the responsibility of your after-life, and take a fierce delight in letting her ever be aware that you have bade a scornful farewell to those sacred sentiments, by the very belief and indulgence in which you strove to win her, long ago? Could I have loved you, be sure I could have loved you only for your virtues and your worth."

"My worth!" he said, laughingly. "You say so, and doubtless say sincerely; but you know neither the universal heart of your sex nor your own. I tell you—what the contents of those drawers could prove—that women are won by everything except our virtues. Had I come in the guise of a mocking Mephistopheles, with a questionable morality and a flippant tongue, I should have won your love, Mary Dormer!— saint though you are, and I know you to be—as I have since won the love of women about whose love I am very silent, because I would fain be rid of it and replace it by that of others as easily got and as poorly prized. If I am not right—tell me, why are you here now? I am no longer the devout boy, praying with you in Onchester fields; you think I am of the lost, and forthwith I am interesting. If not for this reason, why, why do you subject both yourself and me to this?"

"That you are interesting to me, I need not deny; but you were surely that before you learned to sneer at the devout natures of whom you once were one. The woman who can cease to be interested in the welfare of him who once loved her is—I know not what—nay, she is no woman. I do not know if the tone of your language to-night is your habitual tone; it grates on me now, it grated on me that night when you kindly took me home in the cab from the dance where Mr. Chesterfield had left me. I say it was kind of you to take me ; but could I have guessed the pain which your voice, your manner, and your words were going to inflict on me, I would rather, ten thousand times rather, have let everybody know my humiliating position than have appealed to you to save me from it. Do I not remember the Onchester fields as well as you, and all the noble utterances and worthy promises of endeavour that fell from your lips in our pleasant wanderings ? It is to these I would recall you ; it is to yourself that I would recall you. Is it I alone who lament your fall from those lofty aspirations? There travels on the waters this night one who is thinking of you even now, I doubt not — thinking and grieving ; who, were he here, would join his voice to mine. His last words—his only words to me this day were of you ;" she covered her face. "*He* has driven me here ; but it was you who drove him to me."

"Stephen Grafton ?" The truth dawned upon him.

"Yes, yes ! Together can we not move you ?

What am I ?   At most a child, trusting in the
God who is well pleased to send me suffering.
But you—you, Cyril Vavasour !   You have
been sent by Him to do some right noble work,
and you refuse to do it !   Why do I come ?
Why did your friend send me ?   Why, to
snatch you from your own degradation ! "

Earnestness and the love of right guided her
words ; tact would have suggested a different
language.   What ! he was to be *managed* into
a worthier career ?   Quickly he answered :

" You come, then, to snatch me from a degradation I no longer feel.   Sent to do some right
noble work ?   Yes ! I will retort : and *you*
were sent to help me !   And you too, have
refused.   It was in the light of your presence
and your fancied affection—never before, never
since—that I saw what noble work it was.
Who withdrew the light ?   Either God or you
—not I.   I know I have groped—blundered—
my way ever since ; see no work worth doing
—nay, want none.   I have found happiness, or
something so like it that I approve the substitute—happiness in indifference, indifference

even to my own desires when they cannot be gratified without the condition of labour or denial. Do you want me to tell you a third time that I loved you? You say you once believed—once doubted : you doubted me when I paid you the *strange* visit as you were leaving Onchester ; and yet I loved you then far better than when you believed me."

"Pardon me—pardon me! I believe it now. I ought never to have doubted, perhaps; but Love, even in the assumed guise of Friendship, does not usually show itself by an eighteen months' silence."

He was about to speak. "Nay, hear me out," she continued. "I know more now than I knew then; but we will not disturb that knowledge. Sufficient for me if I bring you to think that I am deeply grateful to you for all that you have ever done or shown towards me ; to think that affection for one more removed than a father never surpassed my affection for you ; to think that, had I bestowed what you demanded, you would have had little that was worth having ; to think of me as a kind not a cruel episode in your career, and not to add what bitterness *can* be added to the many griefs of my life, by showing me that I have not only embittered but poisoned yours. Even the peace of a convent will not grant me rest, so long as I am forced to think that outside its walls lives one who was papa's friend, and Reginald's, and mine, and lives unworthily."

" Well, then, carry to your convent what poor consolation I can offer. But know the facts, and then judge me. I think my father from his grave will forgive me for divulging a secret that you will not in your convent be tempted to repeat, and which, indeed, I am sure, whatever the temptation, you will still never betray." The first kind words he had uttered. " You remember how we parted, when I first spoke to you of love. I went home to hear that my father was ruined, leaving me for inheritance —a debt. Since then I have at least maintained myself, if I have been able to do no more. My father died; and by his very grave I was thinking of you—thinking how I might take all the grief, and leave you none. I thought—nay, I was

certain (was I wrong ?) that you—I will not say
loved, but—cared for me. But I felt that time
and absence would easily remove from your
heart the small impression I had made ; and as
for myself, whatever my pain, the circumstances
in which I was placed forbade the thought of
love—at any rate of marriage. So for your
sake, and your sake only, I took refuge in
silence and in time. Twelve months later *your*
papa died. I remember well what I then
underwent, and the letter I wrote poor Reginald. To you I did not write at all, though,
God knows—nay, I will be silent. Of your
circumstances I knew nothing ; but I hoped—
it was the least selfish of hopes—that you had
been left not to need a shelter from me. One
day, in the great city, I heard the sad truth. I
hurried to Onchester ; I saw you : you know
what passed. I thought no poverty could be
so great as to absolve me from the duty of
offering a home, however modest, to the girl
to whom I had once offered my heart, and
who yet possessed it, when she came to be left
without a home at all. Had you been able to

repay me love for love, I should have told you
then what I am telling you now. You could
not so repay me, and there was an end, and
—what has followed since."

His words were so simple and so simply said,
so manly in their truthfulness, so free from all
trace of his predominant scorn, if also free from
all trace of once-heard tenderness, that she stood
and felt arraigned. To her at least he had
acquitted himself, and his acquittal sounded,
though clearly it was not so intended, like accusation of her ; for was there not something
wrong in their fortunes ? . . . Was she to be
silent ?

" I believe all—all ! " she said. " What you
have uttered is the truth, as *you* saw it. Shall
I not tell you what seemed the truth as *I* saw
it ? I surely thought, when we first parted
after your inaugural tenderness to me, that at
least we understood each other. Your father
died : in what circumstances, it did not occur to
me to ask. But I could not fail to ask myself
what was the meaning of your studied estrange-
ment ? What meaned your cautious condolence

when my father died? What meaned your apparent haste to save your honour at the expense of mine, when you shrank from letting the girl, to whom you had once breathed the name of love, sink to what you evidently thought the degraded position of a hired menial? Remember, I speak but of appearances; of things that then seemed to be; I know now, seemed falsely. Forgive me! I was much to blame in that last interview between us at Onchester. Indeed the blame was wholly mine, since I uttered words that must have sounded to you full of scornful reproach, though, verily, with no such feeling were they spoken."

"But, as I afterwards learned, you knew then —*then*," he said, resuming the harshness of his original tone, "that I was little more than a beggar? I know not how you knew it, but know it you did."

"Indeed, no! God forbid! or——"

"Why," he broke in, impatiently interrupting her, "Reginald told me, when I taxed him shortly after with his never coming near me,

that you had cautioned him against allowing
me to be too kind to him, because you knew my
father had died so poor."

She started.

" I did not tell him that—for I did not know
it—till three weeks after the date of which we
speak, the date of your hasty visit. I learned
it from Mr. Morley, and it came upon me with
suddenness and pain."

Vavasour turned aside.

" O Reginald! Reginald! and you told me
this "—he spoke aloud—" as an excuse for your
coldness of the twelve previous months!"

She leaped eagerly at his meaning.

" And you thought that I refused your love
because I knew you to be poor! because I
fancied in a Frank Morley, or whom you will, a
wealthier husband! Cyril, you thought *this* of
me ? Tell me!"

" I thought many things," he answered ; " as
we ever do when we want to save our self-love.
I was willing to think anything except the truth,
that of my own personal demerits I fell short of
winning you. It was an unkind, but perhaps a

pardonable, vanity. Why, even now I am anxious to find for that vanity some retrospective consolation." (He half smiled, half sneered.) "Do you mind telling me whether, at that time to which we refer, if you had not fancied that I came rather with the shame and pity of a misplaced chivalry, than the anxious questioning of a spontaneous love,—whether or not you would have dismissed me as you did ? You do not like to answer. I thought plain words were best when people were about to part. Well, never mind ; let the past remain still uninterpreted or misconstrued. But *I* will answer for you. I believe now that you would not quite so have dismissed me. I never really believed— though I tried hard to believe—that my poverty had a share in my being condemned. I do not in the least believe it. Indeed, I believe that you cared somewhat for me then, or would have cared, had you not been so cautious and suspecting" (he shrugged his shoulders as though he were talking to Blanche Latimer) ; "cared *tant soit peu*,—just a little. But you loved me, at best, but little ; you loved your pride, at the very least, overmuch. And to save your pride, you sent away, and made what you see and hear him, one who I do not shrink from saying was the most believing and bounteous boy who ever flung his future at a maiden's feet."

She stood pale, silent, and absorbed. At last she spoke.

"You say I loved you little, my pride much. Both *your* pride and *your* love shall undergo a similar test. I cast aside the sympathies of my sex: God's ordinances are for all. My grandpapa is dead."

"Dead!"

"Yes, dead. I cannot pretend to mourn him, save that he did not die, as far as human eyes can judge, as Christians should; but God is merciful. He has left me a not large, but a sufficient and a certain, income; more, at least, than it was ever in your power to offer me. But this—my all—which you once offered and I refused, I now offer to you. Will pride or love prevail?"

"What!" he fiercely exclaimed; "you think,

then, that my degradation, of which you spoke, is so deep that I shall not turn even from this new disgrace? No! I am not sunk quite so low as that; not—— "

"It was not money," she said, alarmedly, "that I offered you. I spoke of my *all!*—all that *you* ever offered *me.*"

"Oh, I understand. You will be my wife. And time was when I had rather have called you by that name than have stood immortal in the Land of Light. But now! You offer me what I offered you? You cannot. *You* come with a holy, with a religious pity for a soul that you fancy will be lost, and which you fear you have endangered. To save it, you will sacrifice your own earthly wishes; and this you call all that I ever offered you? Child! I faint for language; but what *I* once offered *you* was an essence so spiritual and subtle, though so intense, that even in offering it, though it was not accepted, I could not again imprison it. You would not receive it, but it has left me; and ever since have I been, and so for

all time shall I remain, without the pulsa-
tions of a heart, without the suggestions of a
soul."

She shook into tears.

" Go, child! go!" he continued ; "let us
part now, but let us part kindly. Your
tears are not tears that I like to see ; taunts
between us are unnatural, and regrets are
worse than useless."

" Oh! say not," she exclaimed, "that regrets
are useless. Regrets are the appendix of the
past, completing our otherwise imperfect labours.
God help me! God help us both! But, happen
what will, the past shall *not* go, either uninterpreted or misconstrued. I loved you
before my presence gave you joy. I shall
love you, Cyril, long after my absence has
ceased to give you pain!"

His heart that, like a disgraced hound, had
slunk away and crouched clandestine from the
sight of his existence, leaped up to the hand
that lured it. Wide opened he his arms, and
into them, as into paradisal gates, she rushed.
His lips all athirst for hers, he kissed her with

the kept-back kisses of the unkind, separating years ; and, lost for language, he could only say, and say, and say again :

"My darling ! my darling !   At last !"

THE END.

BRADBURY AND EVANS, PRINTERS, WHITEFRIARS.